LEASHING THE ALIEN

BEASTLY ALIEN BOSS, BOOK 2

AVA ROSS

LEASHING THE ALIEN

Beastly Alien Boss Series, Book 2

Copyright © 2022 Ava Ross

All rights reserved.

Cover art by Natasha Snow Designs

Editing/Proofreading by Owl Eyes Proofs & Edits & Del's Diabolical Editing

AISN: B09ZZS64C3

✿ Created with Vellum

FOREWORD

A note to the reader.

If you found this book outside of Amazon,
it's likely a stolen/pirated copy.
Authors make nothing when books are pirated.
If authors are not paid for their work,
they can't afford to keep writing.

*For my mom who
always believed in me.*

*And for my dad.
I found your handwritten stories
among your things!
They're amazing.*

SERIES BY AVA

Mail-Order Brides of Crakair

Brides of Driegon

Fated Mates of the Ferlaern Warriors

Fated Mates of the Xilan Warriors

Holiday with a Cu'zod Warrior

Galaxy Games

Alien Warrior Abandoned/
Shattered Galaxies

Beastly Alien Boss

You can find my books on Amazon.

LEASHING THE ALIEN

**I was hired to tame alien pets,
but my beastly alien boss
is determined to tame me.**

As a pet whisperer, I've yet to meet a snarling beast I can't turn into a purring pussycat. When a billionaire alien living in a castle on an isolated planet posts a job looking for someone to housebreak his pets, I'm confident I can train them to eat out of his hand instead of trying to bite his head off.

My growly boss has two rules. Don't touch him and remain inside my room at night. The first part's a challenge, because I have an overwhelming urge to nuzzle his neck and lick . . . his fingers. As for the second, I lie awake all night, struggling to ignore the howls echoing through the barren castle passages.

I might be here to train his pets to walk on a leash, but I'm beginning to suspect there's a beast in this castle who wants to train me.

Leashing the Alien is Book 2 in the Beastly Alien Boss Series. Each book is standalone and features a woman hired for an off-world job who meets a gruff alien who can't resist falling for his fated mate.

1

JENNY

"Dearly beloved, we are gathered here today to bless Jennifer and Thurston Harold Willington the fifth's marriage . . ."

I tried to block out the reverend's words, but they sunk into my skin like battery acid. My cringing glance Thurston's way showed him grinning at me, horrifying lust in his eyes. The second the vows were spoken; he'd drag me to a bedroom and toss me on a bed. Or he'd throw me to the carpet in the hall outside the chapel and consummate this farce of a marriage.

Behind us, the guests watched raptly. My dad, who arranged this horrifying match between me and Thurston's family, kept his finger on his wrist com in warning. One wrong move on my part, and electricity would jolt through me. Not enough to knock me out, but enough to show me who was in charge of this situation.

Tears trickled down Mom's face, probably because

what's happening to me brought back memories of how her and Dad's relationship started.

Forced marriage was a family tradition, and no one had been able to escape its tight grasp.

Thankfully, my father agreed to my request for an outdoor wedding.

And the inclusion of a friend's pet doves.

The reverend beamed benignly at me and Thurston before scanning the gathered audience. "If there is anyone here who protests this union, speak now, or forever hold your peace."

On cue, the doves I'd worked with when my friend first got them flew down the aisle, aiming straight for me and Thurston. I was so grateful, I wanted to cry.

They saw me waiting. And they saw the finger gesture I made, a simple twirl that, to most, would mean nothing. To them, I was asking for the movements we'd practiced.

A pet whisperer, my friends laughingly called me, because I could turn even the most ferocious beast into a tail-wagging pup begging for kisses.

The doves soared up, then split and flew back toward where I waited. While most of the audience cooed in awe, assuming this was part of the service, others stared wide eyed. I held back my grin.

The birds dove toward my father.

He squawked, reeling back with his hands lifting. Titters and shrieks erupted from those gathered, but the birds had only one task in mind: to attack the person holding the controller. I'd practiced this with them for months after my engagement to Thurston was announced. First, I'd used a mannequin, then another friend who thought I was preparing a joke.

The crowd gaped, unsure if they should run or stay to watch the rest of the spectacle.

I kicked Thurston hard in the shin, and he grunted, releasing his hold on my wrist. I ripped away the band strapped to my ankle and flung it toward my father.

Pivoting, I leaped off the dais.

My mother smiled and nodded, and the birds flew toward my friend's house where she'd collect them and hide them from my father.

Thurston bellowed in outrage as I fled down the aisle. At the end, I darted through the archway ornately decorated with flowers, their cloying scent coating my nostrils.

Inside the tiny building attached to the back of the hotel where I prepared for this horrifying event, I grabbed the bag I'd hidden in the back of the closet. I didn't stop to change but wrenched open the outer door and raced into the main part of the hotel. I fled across the lobby and out onto the street.

Behind me, pandemonium reigned, but one shout rang out among them all.

"*Jennifer*," my father roared.

I didn't look back but ran down the street, big city buildings towering over me. My father owned three or four of them. I'd lost track. Five, if we counted the one Thurston gifted dear old Dad after he forced me to agree to this farce of a marriage.

Transport craft flew overhead, the hum of their electric engines barely noticeable above the chatter of a wide variety of aliens striding down the walkway around me. Some lived here; others were tourists from distant planets.

Oh, to be as free as them, to choose where I wanted to go and who I wanted to marry. To be free to live my own life.

"Jennifer," Thurston bellowed behind me. "Get back here."

"No," I hissed. Never again.

I skittered forward, nearly falling when my stupid heel was sucked down into a crack in the concrete. I yanked it off and smacked it on the stone, breaking off the heel. Then the other.

With my billowy white skirts bunched in my hand, I bolted, my bag jostling against my thigh. I didn't have much inside, just a few changes of clothing and the credits I'd skimmed off the trust my grandmother left me —the one my father controlled, though it should've been handed over to me three years ago when I turned twenty-five.

I had nothing else, not even a solid plan. Get to the transport hub and blend in with the crowd, something I couldn't do until I'd found a place to ditch my floofy white gown. I stood out like the topper on a lush wedding cake.

Everyone pointed, and when cries from my father and Thurston grew louder behind me, those watching melted back against the buildings.

A glance over my shoulder showed they were too close. I cringed, worried I wasn't going to get away.

With fear and desperation charging through my veins, I ran faster. I spiraled around one corner and then another, weaving through the city until their cries grew fainter.

I thought I'd escaped them. Then a soft chitter reached my ears. Shit, they'd sent a tracker. If the mechanical bounty hunter locked onto me, I'd never get away.

I peered around, looking for a place to hide.

A sign hanging from a shop just ahead drew my eye. *Intergalactic Employment Agency.*

I didn't need a job, but they might have a back door I could slink through after using their bathroom to change.

When I slammed inside, a bell overheard jangled. Breathing fast, I turned and peered through the plexi, watching as the tracker soared down the street.

Still looking, then. My breath whooshed from me.

"Come for a job, have you?" a female with a crotchety voice said from behind me. "At the Intergalactic Employment Agency, we're determined to place you in the position of your dreams."

Any job was a dream position if Thurston wasn't part of it.

I turned, plastering a smile on my face. "Hi."

"I have to say, we don't get many brides in here," the gray-haired woman said, her pale blue eyes sparkling as she took in my dress and white shoes with snapped-off heels. Thin and a few inches taller than my five-eight, she wore a polka dot dress with a hem swishing across her knees. "But if you're looking for a job that includes marriage, I'll see what I can do."

"No!" I lowered my voice and tried to control my ragged breathing. "No weddings. I'm not actually here for a—"

Outside, the click of the tracker grew louder. If the droid found me, it would secure my wrists and ankles with unbreakable ties and contain me until my father arrived. Thurston would be hot on Dad's heels, eager to consummate our now-defunct wedding vows.

I stepped closer to the woman and, grabbing her arm, led her to the back of the room where the tracker's beams might not reach.

"I don't have a lot of experience," I said. "But I'm excited to hear about whatever you have to offer that *does not* include marriage."

"All right. We'll leave mail-order brides out of the search." Her rheumy gaze darted to my wrist. "You're not wearing your com."

If I was, the tracker would already have me pinned to the sidewalk. A com held all our data, including past work history. I'd told Thurston I didn't want to wear the clunky device for our wedding, that it would ruin the look I was aiming for. Since I simpered and batted my eyelashes when I said it, he believed me.

"I dropped my com into the dishwater this morning," I said breezily. "I need to get a new one. Tell me about the jobs. I'm looking for something outside the city."

"What about off world?" the woman asked. "I'm Faylene, by the way. I don't normally work this shift, but the regular guy called out sick."

"Off-world jobs?" I asked. "That sounds interesting."

"Let me see what I can find for you." Faylene strolled around behind a counter. A universal com lifted from the surface.

She closed her eyes, accessing the device with the chip implanted within her brain. I'd resisted having mine placed, insisting I preferred using a more antiquated com on my wrist. With an implanted device, I'd never hide from my father or Thurston.

"If you'll allow me to access your data the old-fashioned way," Faylene said, staring at the screen.

A probe extended from my side of the computer, and I laid my thumb on the flat surface for the count of three before pulling it away.

"Jennifer Arasteller," Faylene said, a frown forming on her face. "It doesn't appear you've ever held a job, my dear."

"My father is quite strict about that."

Women should never work, he always said. *They should keep busy by caring for their husbands.*

Be controlled, that is.

"I'm a pet whisperer," I said proudly.

Lines appeared on Faylene's brow. "I'm not familiar with that position."

"I can talk animals, creatures, and even beasts into behaving. You've got a hissing pussy cat? I'll make it purr. Even wild dogs eat out of my hand."

Her face cleared. "Ah. Yes. So pet sitting, walking, and care might be job options for you. Let me see." Her eyelids slid closed before popping open. "I have a few off-world positions I can suggest."

"Such as?"

"The Questrians need someone to lead a trail ride into the Veskitan Sector."

Lead a trail ride? Gulp. "What do they ride?"

"Flying kestelars. The trails weave around giant floating islands in the sky."

I didn't mind heights, but . . . "I've never flown on a kestelar before."

"Ah, well. That wouldn't work well for you, then, now would it?" Faylene squinted at the screen. "We also have an opening for an octureet walker in a hootinair."

"What's a hootinair?"

"A harem."

Sounded too close to marriage to Thurston. "Nope."

"When one lacks experience, one can't be picky," Faylene said with a twist of her lips. "However, I have one other position I can offer. A wealthy businessman living on a remote planet has adopted two culair pups and it says here . . ." She leaned closer to the screen. "He's finding them a bit of a challenge."

What was a culair?

A clicking sound erupted behind me, and a glance through the plexi showed the tracker hovering outside the door, its seeking beam skimming back and forth across the floor, coming this way. Damn, it would find me. Would it enter the business or wait for me to emerge? I couldn't stay inside forever.

"You wouldn't happen to have a back door, would you?" I asked. I'd find someplace else to change.

"We do not," she said, her gaze taking in the tracker. "What is a—"

"Awesome," I bellowed, making her jump. "I'll take the job."

Faylene's head tilted, and she frowned at the bag hanging from my arm. "Would you like to go home and pack? I can send a shuttle for you tomorrow."

"I'd like to leave immediately."

"Dressed like that?"

"Wedding dresses are the latest fashion. Everyone's using them for daily wear."

"Why would they do something like that?" Faylene asked, tapping her chin. "I sense something unusual about this transaction."

That was an understatement.

The tracker rammed against the door. My skin jolted, and my heart beat furiously against the lace bodice of my dress.

"I need to leave now," I said, rushing around the counter to grab Faylene's arm. "Please."

She shook her head, making her low bun quiver. "All right." With a tug away from my grasp, she stepped backward. "I'll call for a shuttle immediately." A pinch of her eyes, and a rumble rang out in the back of the room.

When the pod hit the floor with a thud, the plexi hatch opened.

"I'll notify Vengestire that you'll be arriving," Faylene said.

"Vengestire?"

"Your new employer, Vengestire Rarkeleone Abesteen."

"Thanks." While the tracker banged on the front door, I hurried over to the pod and stepped inside. Talk about a tight escape. "How long will I travel before I arrive?"

"It will take three lunar eclipses of this planet to reach Darkfire. But you'll remain in stasis."

"Darkfire?"

"It's a small planet in the Westula Quadrant. There are only a few residents in the town area, but this is a short-term position, and I doubt you'll have much time to miss bustling city life. You'll be back here before you know it."

If I were lucky, I'd never return to Earth. I had no idea where I'd go after this job finished, but I'd have time to plot a trailless escape. Once I'd found a secure location, I could begin the process of wrestling control of my trust away from my father. "Darkfire sounds lovely."

I dropped my bag by my feet and straps wound around my arms and thighs to hold me in place.

As the pod lid sealed, locking me inside, Faylene waved goodbye and grinned.

I had to wonder what I was getting myself into.

But anything was better than marrying Thurston.

2
VENGE

My cry of pain echoed around me, as did the clink of the chains pinning me to the wall.

I shifted, and bangs from my rigid body impacting with the stone surface rang out in the room. My leathery stone wings dug into the granite, leaving grooves.

Soon, dawn would come, and this would be over—until the next night and the one after that.

Until I no longer returned to myself in the morning.

Was there no end for this, or would I wallow within this nightmare forever?

With a snarl ripping from my throat, I ducked, barely avoiding being incinerated by my newly adopted pets. Leaping, I flung myself over the sofa. I rolled across the wood floorboards and came up to a crouch, watching as the two culair pups stalked toward me. When they glanced at each other, I lunged to the corner and grabbed one of the many nets on poles I'd scattered throughout my castle.

Fleese, the smartest of the two culair pups narrowed his eyes on the net. I'd only caught him once, and that was enough for him to learn what I could do with the device.

He chittered to his brother, Gular, and they split, scampering around either side of the sofa, before racing toward me across the open area of my main living room.

The door to the room remained open. If I could get through and shut it, I could escape their attack this time.

While I slowly eased around the right side of the room, aiming for the door, Fleese darted in my direction, hoping to cut me off.

I lifted the net, showing him I meant business. After a harsh burn on my arm, I'd learned their tricks—some of them, that is.

With a bellow, I pivoted and raced to my left, jumping through the doorway while a blast of flames lit across the area where I'd just been standing. I'd already fireproofed the first floor of the castle, so the flames wouldn't burn the place down. Scrapes of their claws rang out behind me as they gave up stalking and galloped after me.

I slid the panel closed with a bang. The culair's howls of dismay echoed in the big room as they added more grooves to the back of the door. They scratched for a short time before going silent. If I knew them—and I'd learned many lessons over the past lunar cycle—they stalked the room, seeking a way out. Then they'd chase me through the castle until I escaped to another level they couldn't reach. So far, they hadn't figured out stairs . . .

I'd already barred all the windows on the second, third, and fourth floors, so they couldn't get to me through that route. As far as I could tell, they couldn't climb higher.

The ceiling above me had been reinforced. Short of clawing through the walls, they were stuck inside this room until I, or my staff member, Ressard, released them.

It was a game for them, and while I'd laughed at their antics at first, I'd soon come to realize they meant business. Would they do more than singe my skin if they caught me?

I didn't want to find out.

I'd been a fool to believe I could find friendship with adopted culairs. My time was ticking down, and I'd have to leave them.

Still, I wouldn't give up yet. In their eyes, I sensed the same need within me, a chance to love another.

I slumped against the wall, though I truly wanted to stomp my feet and swear at the door. Patience, I counseled myself. I couldn't lose control, or I'd be shunned all over again.

My aunt, Azareela, thought I should keep Fleese and Gular penned out back all the time, but how could I do something like that? I knew what it was like to be trapped, and I'd never do that to another being, let alone the creatures I still wanted to befriend.

My only hope was that the pet trainer I'd hired could persuade them to tolerate me.

Without them, I'd have no one.

The trainer was expected to arrive today before nightfall. There wasn't much time left; the sun hovered above the horizon. If she came after the sun set, Azareela would have to greet her and show her to her rooms.

Because the coordinates I'd given would deliver her to my front lawn, I left my house and strode down the long, sloping stone walkway. I climbed the steps of the gazebo I'd built in the center of the lawn after I arrived here many lunar cycles ago and settled on the wide wooden bench.

Fleese and Gular watched me through the plexi panes, their glowing red eyes flaring. They were angry they couldn't reach me.

I sighed. There was nothing new about that.

Earth was sending a female trainer, and I wasn't sure what I thought about sharing this barren crater of a planet with someone else, if only for a brief time. I was raised by Azareela after my mother shunned me, and she'd kept me isolated from others. She and Ressard were the only ones who came to this planet with me. Azareela because she couldn't bear not to be here, Ressard because of the task he would complete at my end.

Surely this female wouldn't expect me to entertain her? My business kept me busy during the day, and I didn't have time to cater to anyone else. At night . . .? Well, I wouldn't even be able to speak to her then.

Her role was to tame my culairs so they'd accept me

into their lives. Other than that, we could ignore each other until she left.

I'd researched these pets for ages. Culairs were intensely loyal, especially if they bonded to their owner within the first few moons of their lives. I only had a few weeks left before that time had passed.

I wasn't sure what I'd do if they rejected me, though I expected it. My own mother had; why not them as well? If I couldn't work with them, I'd find a way to give them a life they'd enjoy that didn't include me.

A hum overhead told me the shuttle was arriving.

I stood, nervous for a reason I couldn't define.

The craft touched down, and a low hiss erupted as it settled, before it went still.

I swallowed hard and left the gazebo, approaching the space pod.

The lid opened and a whoosh of air erupted. Silence ruled after that, until someone inside groaned.

I moved closer, unsure what to do or say.

A person sat up inside the pod and looked around. She rubbed her face and groaned.

"Talk about space lag," the human huffed.

No, she had a name. *Jennifer.* Her dark hair hung down her back, and she wore a rather formal ivory shirt, though the bottom of her outfit must be more sedate. Slight of build, she had an oval face and medium tan skin, so different from my blue skin with tiny plated sections that had evolved through many prior generations to provide my ancestors protection during battle.

She was tiny, as well. When she stood, I doubted the top of her head would come to my mid-chest.

Her height didn't matter, I reminded myself. Neither did her appearance. She was here to do a job and the sooner she did it and left, the better off we'd both be.

She grabbed onto the side of the pod and hefted one leg up and over the edge. Her ivory clothing continued to her feet in one solid item. A gown? Why would a pet trainer wear something like this when traveling to a new job?

Curious to see her face, I moved closer.

She leaned over the side, hitching up her other leg. When she started to tumble, I leapt forward and caught her.

The exposed skin on my hands glided across her arm, and electricity bolted through me, up my arms and across my chest. I couldn't see the center of my chest through my clothing, but I didn't need to look to know what I'd find.

A korier symbol would have appeared. I'd heard of them, naturally. Everyone had spoken of them, wished for them. I'd never expected one to appear on me.

It burned, spreading heat through my body.

I peered down at Jennifer. No, I *snarled* at Jennifer. Before I did something stupid, like kiss her or stroke her face, I placed her on the scorched grass and backed away, my hands lifting.

I rubbed the place on my chest that still stung.

This lowly human female was my fated mate, and I would burn for her forever.

3
JENNY

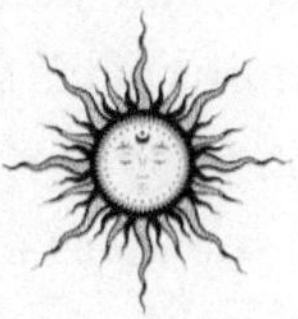

"Ugh," I groaned, rubbing my face. I swore I'd fallen out of the shuttle, but my body didn't hurt from smacking onto the ground. Had I landed on something soft?

I tried to lever myself upright, encountering a solid, firm surface covered in brittle vegetation.

"Get back in that shuttle and leave," someone snarled from nearby. "Don't touch me again. Not only that, but the sun is setting, and you need to be gone from here before it's fully dark."

I ignored the don't-touch part, which I must've misheard. "I just got here. Why do I have to leave?"

"Because I said so."

Squinting, I took in the black leather boots and equally black pants encasing the two legs of someone standing near me. I lifted my gaze, my eyes widening at the white, billowy shirt the alien male wore. If I were the gushing kind, I'd be swooning about his thick thighs, narrow waist, and heavily muscled torso—what I could see outlined by his shirt, that is. He'd rolled up his sleeves, and was I the only one in the world who adored muscled forearms?

Patterned dark blue skin peeked from where he'd undone the top few buttons of his shirt.

Long, golden hair hung down his back, drifting out away from his body in the breeze. I shouldn't be turned on by the idea of a guy with hair as long as mine. I'd just escaped a forced marriage. The last thing I wanted was to start a new relationship.

But all I could picture was him above me, his hair tickling my naked body.

"Hold on," I said. "No tickling."

His brows lifted. "Excuse me?"

"Forget I said that." I used the side of the shuttle to climb to my feet, reaching inside to snag my bag. I turned back to the alien. "I assume you're my new boss?"

"I said, you need to leave," he bit out in a snooty tone.

I sighed. Truly, I'd put up with a lot of crap from Thurston. He had money. He loved his money. He only wanted to be with me because my money would double his money.

Everyone around him must serve a purpose—making him more money—or they'd be surgically removed from his life.

This alien gave off the same vibe.

"I came here to tame a couple of pets. Unless this is

the wrong planet?" I said. In some ways, I hoped it was, because whoa. How was I going to hang around a boss who looked like him and focus on work?

"I have pets in need of taming, but it must be done by someone else."

His rejection made a bitter taint coat the top of my tongue.

"Is it the girl thing," I pinched the skirt of my gown to flare it, "or how I'm dressed? I assure you; I'll ditch the wedding gown as soon as possible and wear sensible jeans from now on."

"Leave." He pivoted on his heel and started striding across a big, scraggly grass lawn. Either it rarely rained here, and no one watered, or the sun was hot, and it scorched the surface of the planet.

An enormous black structure loomed beyond him.

Whoa, castle. The multi-storied thing rose toward the clouds beyond him, complete with a moat and a drawbridge. The castle appeared to be constructed of lava rock, though I must be mistaken.

I hooked my bag over my arm and hurried after him, my stupid white shoes crunching on the gravel walk. "Are you Vengestire?"

"I am, but why have you not left?" He didn't turn, just barked over his shoulder. "It will be dark soon. You need to be gone from this place before that time."

I took the chance to check out his butt. He might be demanding, but he was decent to look at. Scorching, actually.

"You've got a tail," I said, wishing I could take back the words. It was never nice to talk about someone else's body parts. But I couldn't seem to help it. "I like the fluffy tip."

I caught up and walked beside him.

"Why are you not doing as I demand?" he clipped out.

"Because I'm here to do a job, and I'm not leaving until I finish."

He groaned but kept walking. "I do not wish to speak with you."

"Then why did you hire me?" When he outpaced me, I fisted my skirt to keep from tripping over it and picked up my pace to a jog. "It's the girl thing, isn't it? You just don't want to admit it." I tapped his arm to get his attention, touching his shirt, not his skin—though I was tempted. Those forearms!

He stopped abruptly and faced me. "I remind you again. Do. Not. Touch. Me."

"That's fair enough. I won't."

Man was he mad, though it couldn't be from something as simple as the light tap on his arm. I swore, if he could make it happen, steam would erupt from his nostrils and ears. Well, maybe he could. I took a step backward just in case.

"You're going to have a heart attack if you keep that up," I said.

"Excuse me?" He glared down his long but rather cute nose at me.

"It's not good to let anger rule you. It messes with your blood pressure and before you know it, you'll have chest pain. If you have vascular issues, you'll drop over from cardiac arrest."

"You make no sense."

"Do you want to explain why you're so upset?" I was still convinced he was rejecting me because I was female. He'd fumble around, trying to find an excuse that would fit, but my sex would be glaringly obvious. I propped my fist on my hip. "You need to know right now that I'm not only capable of doing this job, but I'm also the best pet whisperer in the universe."

He snorted. "This has nothing to do with you being female."

So they all said.

"The reason I need you to leave is because you have sparked my korier. Once you have departed, I will find a way to ignore it."

"What's a korier?"

He peered down at me with penetrating, deep purple eyes. The contrast between them and his dark blue skin was kind of cool. I noticed this in an abstract way. "It means you are fated to be with me."

I reeled away from him. "Just because I'm dressed as a bride, it doesn't mean I'm eager to hook up with anyone."

"I will never propose something like that." He stalked past me, leaving the crushed stone path, and striding up onto the wooden drawbridge.

"Good, because I wouldn't accept," I shouted to his back.

He stopped but didn't turn, his fists clenching at his sides. "Leave now."

"What if I want to stay?" This korier shit had sparked my curiosity. I ignored the belonging to him comment. He had to be mistaken. "There's no reason we need to interact outside of my job. I won't touch you, and I won't mess with your korier. I'll train them to walk on a leash before you know it."

"I need you to train them to like me."

That was an odd comment. Usually when I worked with pets, I taught them to use the litter box, walk well on a leash, come when called rather than leap away whenever their owners got near, and general behavior management. Like, not jumping up onto counters and eating an entire cake.

Loving a pet and being loved in return wasn't an issue I'd run into before.

"You're not mean to them, are you?" If he was, I'd bail on this job fast, taking the culairs with me.

His spine stiffened, and his tail whipped back and forth behind him. "I would never be cruel to another creature."

That eased my tension. "All right. That's good."

"I will work with them myself." He finished crossing the bridge and strode up to a huge bronze double front door. Opening the one on the right side with a broad sweep of his arm, he stepped inside.

Not willing to be left behind with the sun going

down, I trotted behind him, joining him inside a huge foyer with a ceiling that looked like it went all the way to the roof. Doors led to other parts of the castle on either side, plus the back wall. A broad, carpeted staircase spiraled up through the center, exiting to landings on each floor. My belly would plunge into the ground, and I'd have a hard time holding onto my meals if I looked down while climbing those stairs.

Paintings of dour-faced aliens of Vengestire's species peppered the walls of the foyer, but other than a few tall urns and a thick, dark-patterned rug beneath my feet, the room was empty.

"Why hire a trainer and pay the expense of having her shipped here if you don't need her help?" I asked.

He growled and spun around to face me. "They hate me. *You* will soon hate me. You will beg for me to send you home."

I chuckled. He had to be joking about the culairs. "They're pets. I'm sure you're misreading them."

"You've worked with this species before?" His penetrating gaze met mine before sliding down my front.

I shouldn't feel hot and bothered by his assessment, but I did.

"I haven't exactly worked with culairs," I said, my chin lifting. "Yet! But I've tamed more creatures than I can count."

He huffed.

For a guy stating I was fated to be with him, he wasn't making much effort to be pleasant.

As for the fated comment, I brushed that aside. He

didn't appear to be eager to act on it and, as long as kept his hands to himself, we'd get along fine.

I didn't need a happy attitude on his part to do this job. As soon as I'd tamed his culairs, I'd leave.

Because I was worried I might start thinking this fated stuff was real.

4
VENGE

Why wasn't she leaving? I'd told her to go. Instead, she followed me across my bridge and through the front door of my castle.

I needed to get away from her before I . . .

"I will not house you. I will not feed you," Anything to get her to leave. Even now, the symbol on my chest rippled. The mate bond pheromones were dumping into my bloodstream, and if I didn't get away from her soon, it would be too late. The bond would solidify, and I'd never want her to leave.

She was an employee. The last thing I needed to do was grab her, shred her clothing, then press my naked body against hers.

A growl ripped from my throat.

She jumped and turned a wide-eyed gaze my way. "Indigestion?"

"You really must leave."

Azareela sidled up behind Jennifer.

"Could you please tell him I will escort you to your quarters?" Azareela said. She didn't make eye contact with me, but there was nothing new about that. Devastated by what was happening to me, she said it hurt to speak with me at all.

"Excuse me?" Jennifer said. Her hand jutted out. "I'm Jenny, by the way."

"Azareela." My aunt nodded. "Please tell him I will escort you to your quarters."

"Him. I assume you're talking about Vengestire, a name which is a lot to digest in one bite, so I'm going to call him Venge."

"Who else would I speak of but him?"

"Then ask him yourself," Jenny said.

"I cannot."

Jenny sighed. "This makes absolutely no sense."

"I agree," I said.

She turned a sassy gaze my way. "I should be irritated by your behavior—"

Azareela huffed.

"But I'm going to call it nervousness on your part," Jenny continued.

"I am not nervous," I bellowed.

She smirked. "Are you constipated, then?"

Azareela backed away from us both.

"You need to leave," I yelled. "It will be dark soon."

"Why? Do you turn into a vampire when the sun goes down?"

I had no idea what she meant. "You need to be gone from my sight before it is too late."

"So, you've got a sundown issue," Jenny said, rubbing her hands together. "I'll find a way to deal with it. Let's get back to the job."

"There is no job for you here," I grumbled.

"You need to give me a chance to prove I can do this. I'll tame your culairs in no time, and you'll be happy with my service," she said. "*Then* I'll leave." She nodded as if that settled things between us and moved closer to Azareela. "Perhaps you should take me to my room before Venge here turns into mist and drifts away like a puff of smoke."

I gnashed my teeth.

A door opened at the opposite end of the foyer, and Ressard strode through, his gaze trained on me.

"You must come with me now," he barked. "Hurry."

He was right. It was too late to force Jenny to leave. She must not see me once the sun had set.

Azareela snatched at Jenny's sleeve, holding tight. "We must leave him before . . ."

"What is going on?" Jenny asked, peering between the three of us.

"Nothing you need to know about. Come. I will lead you to your room," Azareela said, not looking my way. "You may call me Azareela. Tell him I will see him in the morning. Tell him that the shuttle you arrived in has departed."

"Oh, it has? Bummer about that." Jenny didn't sound too upset. She glanced at me. "I don't understand why she's not speaking directly with you. Did you two squabble?"

I grumbled, not feeling a need to explain myself to her. "Sometimes she chooses not to unless there is dire need. I do not understand it myself."

I'd accepted that this was the way it needed to be.

Azareela backed toward the stairs, her hands lifting as if she'd need to defend herself against my wrath. I rarely directed it at her. She must know I saved it for myself alone.

"I don't understand. Did you kill someone?" Jenny quipped, but her teasing smile faded when my expression went grim.

"Nothing like that." I might become a monster at night, but so far, I had not harmed another. If I tried, they would kill me.

"Oh, shit." Jenny's fingers trembled against her lips. "Let me guess. I've read a ton of fantasy books. You're a cursed lord living on this barren planet in a lava stone castle. You were banished here because you did something horrible . . . I don't know what, but I'll figure it out. Only after you've done your time will you be freed."

Azareela stared at Jenny with a mix of fascination and horror.

"Do my time?" I asked, picking that bit out of her ramblings. Her words were too close to comfort for my taste.

"Once you've done your penance, you can . . . go back to wherever you came from."

"I am originally from the planet Brex'an."

"Yes, you'll be able to return to Brex'an." She nodded pertly, and despite my unwillingness to be drawn into her thrall, I couldn't seem to resist. She called to me like a testilar to a blossom. One taste of her honegge, and I'd be unable to stay away.

"Tell him I will bring a tray to your room this evening," Azareela told Jenny. "I will make sure you will dine there and do not leave until morning."

"Maybe I want to dine with Venge," Jenny said.

I liked the shortened name she'd given me. It suited me since I struggled not to give into vengeance.

"This is a fairytale, isn't it?" Jenny said, a smile twitching across her lips. "I mean, not a *real* one, but something like it. You're the beast of the castle, and you're waiting for someone to save you."

I growled. "I am not a beast." Not completely. "I do not need to be saved." Oh, but I did. She just wasn't the one who could do it. No one could. I was doomed to face my fate alone.

"I'll be with you in a second," Jenny told Azareela. She stalked back to me and grinned up at me. "Never fear. I'm here to help you tame your culairs, and I promise, if there's saving to be done, I'll fit that into my schedule too."

While I sputtered, thrown off by this female once more, she turned and hurried back to Azareela.

"I have a room upstairs?" she said, tipping her head back. "Please tell me it's not in the tower and that I don't have to let down my hair to get free."

Azareela blinked a few times before starting up the stairs. "Follow me."

With a quick smile my way, Jenny continued after Azareela, chattering all the while.

"So, tell me more about Venge," she said.

"You will not speak of me or my past," I commanded as Ressard descended. Thankfully, he kept the ropes behind his back. I had a feeling Jenny wouldn't leave if she knew he planned to take me to the lowest level and chain me to a wall. The thought of which made me both horrified and sad.

"Tell him I speak of whatever I please," Azareela told Jenny.

I huffed, growled, and stomped my feet, but they ignored me, climbing higher.

"Not looking down," Jenny said. "Not looking down." She peered over the rail. "Looking down." Her gaze met mine. "You're watching us."

"I am not," I snarled as Ressard crept closer.

"Why are you wearing such an odd dress?" Azareela asked, tugging Jenny away from the rail.

"This old thing?" Jenny said, pinching the skirt and swishing it. "I was going to get married today, but I decided to run away instead."

"No . . ." Azareela gasped.

"Yup," Jenny said as they continued up the staircase. "Thurston is a fiend, and he's only after my money, so I took the opportunity to leave him at the altar."

Azareela gulped and clutched her hand to her throat. "Will he come after you?"

"I hope not."

They left the staircase, entering the hall on the twelfth floor, but their voices echoed behind them.

"If Thurston follows me here," Jenny said. "I'll haul one of those swords off the wall downstairs and impale him."

No, it would be me impaling anyone who tried to force Jenny to marry them.

Or I'd unleash my beast.

Ressard sighed and lifted the ropes. I didn't fight as he bound my wrists and tethered my ankles to keep me from running. I didn't bellow like usual as he dragged me toward the back staircase.

All I wanted was to keep Jenny from discovering the creature I would soon become.

5
JENNY

Before Azareela and I left the stairwell for a long hall, Venge had sent me a look I couldn't define, though I sensed pain and dismay simmering in his eyes.

And longing. For what, I couldn't be sure. Not me. He'd made it plain he didn't want me here, which meant he didn't want *me*.

No problem. I was used to rejection. My money was my sole draw, per Thurston and all his friends. I was too boring, too mouthy, too—

"Come quickly," Azareela said, leading me down the hall. Thick, pale gray carpet squished beneath my shoes, and widely spaced, closed doors lined both sides of the corridor.

"Tell me about Venge," I said.

"He will share what he chooses," Azareela said in a lofty tone. She was almost Venge's height, though much less bulky. Her blue skin was a shade lighter than his, but she had his same purple eyes with the same penetrating gaze. Her tail jutted from the back of her skirt, sweeping back and forth behind her like a lion's as she walked. Black boots jutted from beneath, and her simple tunic was so pristinely white, it nearly gleamed. Her dark purple hair had been pulled up in a knot on the back of her head, and whenever she looked my way, she flashed one-inch fangs in a tight smile.

"How far off was I by my fantasy novel guess?" I asked.

"He will have to tell you everything himself," she said again. "It is not my place."

I suppose I didn't need to know everything about my new boss to work with him. My goal was to tame the culairs, to make them get along with Venge. I didn't need to know his complete history to do something like that.

"I still think I should eat downstairs with him," I said as Azareela opened a door on the right, midway down the hall.

"That is not possible." Azareela entered a large bedroom ahead of me.

"Why? Doesn't he eat?"

"Not with anyone else, and never with someone after dark." A shudder traveled through her body.

"I'm really beginning to worry about Venge." All of them were holding something back.

I was the curious sort. I wouldn't let this go. If there were secrets to be unveiled inside the castle, I'd expose them to the light of day—so to speak.

I took in the room. A door exited on the right.

"That is the bathing chamber," Azareela said, waving in that direction.

Windows spanned the entire far wall, overlooking an enormous forest made up of pale pink and deep golden trees. Bits of blue spotted the woods, and when they moved, I realized they must be small creatures. Cool.

Turning, I leaned against the windowsill. "Have *you* interacted with the culairs?"

She patted the bed. "You should be comfortable here." She waved to the closets lining an inner wall. "You may place your things there."

"I only brought a few changes of clothing."

"If you're here for long, we will synthesize more for you, naturally."

"I was thinking it'll take me a week, tops."

"You haven't met the culairs," Azareela said.

"They're pets. Show them some love and make your needs clear, and they tend to behave."

"It will be interesting to watch you interact with them." She strode to the door, but her hand stilled on the knob. "Remain inside tonight. Do not attempt to leave."

"This place is amazing. I'm eager to stroll around and check it out."

"I will send a tray soon." She left the room, shutting the door behind her.

I flopped on the bed, pleased that it was big and squishy, though firm enough at the base to support me. I stared at the canopy overhead bedecked with dark fabric. After all the cryptic statements, and if I didn't know better, I'd think I'd stepped into a vampire vid.

Vampires did exist, though not like those in ancient Earth lore. Blood drinkers were just one of the many alien species we'd encountered since interstellar travel became a thing over a hundred years ago.

I slid off the bed and walked to the door. Exploring at least this level of the castle would spark my appetite before dinner. I'd make sure I was back inside my room before anyone arrived.

But when I tried to turn the knob, I found it locked.

6

VENGE

Many lunar cycles had passed since I'd arrived at this castle. My new home. My final home.

Pain blurred my nights and suffering had consumed me since the change had come upon me.

My ancestor's curse. Many generations ago, long before written time, a male in my family played with things he shouldn't have. It forced a change upon him, and the son of every third generation after also succumbed to this . . . curse. It wasn't a magical thing, but one fed by science, though no one could explain why it persisted. Genetic? Or so we assumed.

There was no escaping our fate.

My fate since I was the son of the most recent third generation.

Like every other time the beast possessed me at sundown, I struggled to break free of the chains locking me to the wall of a stark room deep within the bowels of the castle. Stone walls. Stone ceiling. Stone floor.

Stone me.

I'd read lore from every planet I could find, hoping to find an answer. I'd poured through the castle's library, hoping one of my ancestors had left some sort of guidance, though I hadn't found a thing that would help.

Something from Earth tales gave me an answer to what I was becoming.

I was slowly turning into a gargoyle. I'd latched onto the scraps of information I read. A being made of stone. Some believed it protected the building where it resided. Others believed it was pure evil. Had one of my ancestors traveled to Earth and fostered the legends?

At night, I changed, each shift bringing me closer to a being I despised.

Chaotic evil. A sentient being full of cunning and malevolence.

Whenever the beast took over, I was consumed with a need for something I couldn't define. I craved it more each night.

I'd slowly been molding into this horror for many lunar cycles. When they discovered that my fate had caught up to me, who could blame my family for making me leave my home planet to come here? It was what all of us were forced to do.

And after what I'd nearly done . . .

It wasn't murder. Never that. So far, I'd maintained enough control to keep this part of me from taking over completely, though I had begun to lose hope I could hold out much longer.

Like all those of my family who'd also succumbed to

the gargoyle trapped inside them, my people banished me.

I'd been locked within this castle for more lunar cycles than I liked to admit. I'd only dared travel one time to claim the culairs and only then in a ship used to transport prisoners, one with a barred cell.

Perhaps I was a fool to seek pets, but I hated being alone. I'd hoped they could make my last days special.

As with every ancestor who'd lived here, my staff locked me up each night. Ressard's family had performed this task for many generations, almost from the start. He'd do this for the rest of my days on this cursed planet.

With each lunar cycle, I worried I'd sink further into the beast and lose whatever remained of myself.

Straining against the chains, I bellowed and shrieked. I needed to be free. I needed . . .

I shook my head, my sweaty hair dragging across my shoulders. I was naked other than a cloth around my waist to cover my groin. If I didn't remove my clothing when it started, I'd rip it away. My skin itched as it hardened. Only rubbing against the stone kept me from clawing it to shreds.

I didn't know what I needed to do to fix this. I'd consulted every doctor and healer from one end of the galaxy to the other, as had those who'd come before me. I'd hoped someone had missed something that would keep this from claiming me.

The beast was extra restless tonight, which made fear spike through me. Was my full change near?

No. I wasn't ready. I had more things I wanted to do —a silly notion since I'd never have the chance to do them.

Why the sudden shift of my beast? What was different since last night?

She'd arrived.

The korier symbol burned on my chest, drawing my mind away from where it had stepped out to meet the beast. Peering down, I took in the licks of fire swirling around the edges of the design that most would think had been etched into my skin by a master.

No, it had been etched by *Jenny*.

I wasn't sure what it meant. Why would someone like me be gifted with a korier mate if I'd rip her apart one day?

No. I could control this. I would not hurt her. Already, she felt precious to me, a foolish notion since I'd only recently met her. But something inside of me recognized her as mine.

It was clear she wouldn't leave and despite me telling her she had to go, I wanted her to stay. I would not make demands any longer. I would watch and see how this turned out.

I must trust that her work with the culairs would bring them closer to me, that being with them could help me hold off the beast lurking inside me.

Otherwise, I'd be better leaving the castle. Leaving her. I could run into the forest and keep going until I forgot who she was.

The burn of the change roared through me again, a fire I couldn't extinguish, though I tried. Oh, how I tried. It worked its way up my throat, cauterizing my flesh. Tipping my head back, I bellowed in pain.

7
JENNY

So, there wasn't a lock that could keep me inside.

My father learned this when I was twelve, and Thurston within two weeks of our forced engagement. If I wanted out, I found a way.

Hence the ankle shocker.

However, I wasn't being held prisoner inside the castle; there must be a reason they locked the door to my room. Maybe whoever screamed in pain roamed the halls at night and might . . . bite.

Creeped out at the thought of running into the castle ghost, I tried to stay in the room, to wait for someone to bring my dinner. Pacing, I tried to behave when I was tempted to find something sharp to insert into the back of the lock. If I jimmied it loose, I could run.

But the low tortured cries sunk into me, and I was unable to resist their lure.

I dressed in pants and a top quickly, temped to throw the dress out the window, but I didn't have much to wear, and I might need it. I could slice off the skirt and call it a cocktail dress.

"Time to find out what's going on," I whispered.

When I was unable to pick the lock—damn high-tech electronic thing—I strode into the connecting bathroom I'd already determined connected only to this room. No harm in looking twice.

But other than a window inside the smaller space, there was no way out. And twelve floors were a long fall to the ground.

With a huff, I returned to the room and rushed to one of the larger windows, where I lifted the panel.

Beyond a scraggly, burnt lawn that looked like it hadn't been mowed in years, a thick forest stretched for miles in every direction. Other than the craggy hill where this big castle perched, the planet appeared to be covered with dark blue woods.

Within the trees, something howled. Its cry was echoed by others until a chorus of yips and mournful yelps filled the air.

But they were unlike whatever screamed within the castle.

My skin prickled, and I was tempted to close the window, lock it tight, and hide beneath the blankets in the big, lush bed until dinner was served.

Another bellow echoed from somewhere below me.

In the forest, the beasts stilled.

My breath caught. Since I'd noted the cries were louder when I stood near the door, I concluded they came from within, not outside.

I poked my head out the window opening. A ledge spanned the wall of the castle below this bank of windows. Leaning out farther, I peered up, noting this room was only one story below the roof. If I stretched on my tippy toes, I could reach the edge. I was no ninja, but years of daring escapes had toned my muscles and taught me the parameters of what my body could do.

Numerous towers of various heights jutted up from the slate roof.

This was an alien planet, one seemingly barren of other people.

Why would someone build this castle in the middle of nowhere? Maybe I'd find out with a little snooping.

"Now or never," I whispered, hitching one leg out the window. The other followed. I sat on the edge for a bit, trying not to look down. Climbing out the window of the top floor of a two or three-story building was a lot different from this. I was twelve stories up in the air. I'd splat on the ground if I fell. Venge wouldn't be able to scrape enough of me off the stone to ship back to my parents.

I lowered my feet onto the ledge, testing it first before giving it all my weight. From outside, I could see farther on each side. Could I make it to a window in one of the other rooms? I doubted they locked them all.

It was worth a try.

I'd started inching to my right when someone knocked on my bedroom door.

My heart surged up into my throat as I scampered back inside. I smoothed my shirt, though it wasn't wrinkled or hitched up. The motion allowed me a second to calm my nerves.

"You may enter," I called out breezily as I sat on the edge of the bed. My legs were shakier than I'd believed. I wouldn't want anyone to know what I was up to.

A hum resounded, followed by a click.

The door opened, and Azareela strode inside. Her gaze didn't meet mine as she crossed the room and placed the tray on the desk. Turning, she strode to the middle of the room and looked around. She lifted my wedding gown off the chair where I'd laid it. "Would you like me to have this cleaned?"

"If you can. And if someone's handy with a needle and thread, they could shorten it for me."

"There is no one here but me, you, my nephew Vengestire, and Ressard, the groundskeeper."

"Venge is your nephew?"

"I said that, did I not?"

Biting down on my lower lip, I nodded.

"As for this dress," she lifted it higher, frowning at the hem, "Why would anyone use anything as antiquated as a needle and thread? We have a synthesizer that will not only craft clothing for you, but it can also alter the garment."

"That would be wonderful."

Azareela smoothed her fingers across the silky fabric. "I cannot believe you chose to take a position here instead of getting married."

"He wasn't the right guy."

"Marriages are for forming alliances, not choosing someone we wish to be with."

I tilted my head, watching her face. Did I see pain flash there?

"Are you married?" I asked.

"I am not." Her gaze swept the room with scorn. "How could I maintain a marriage in this place?"

I shrugged. "There's always Ressard." I wasn't referring to Venge. For whatever reason, I didn't like the idea of him being with anyone. It was a mean thought. Everyone deserved happiness.

"I cannot imagine marrying Ressard. Perhaps, one day, I will return to my home planet, and then I can mate."

"What's keeping you here?"

"I came here to be with my nephew. I raised him. I love him. Until my task is finished, and . . . Never mind that. I will remain here until this is over."

"Until what is over?"

"Nothing."

She meant anything but nothing, but it was clear I wouldn't be able to pry the information from her tightly compressed lips.

What a sad existence, however. "You don't even speak directly to Venge. Why bother to stay here?"

"I do speak with him on occasion. This is how it must be."

"What did you do before I came here? If no one speaks to him directly, how do you communicate?"

She huffed. "We find a way."

The low, mournful cry echoed within the castle again.

"When are you going to explain *that* to me?" I asked.

"Never." She crossed the room and lowered the window, securing it tight. "Don't open the windows at night. It's not safe."

After hearing the howls, I wasn't sure it was any safer inside the castle than out.

"What did your parents have to say about you choosing not to marry?" she asked, still facing the window. She traced a finger along the sill.

"I didn't ask. I ran."

"And came here?" she asked.

"It's a job and an escape for me. I won't be returning to marry Thurston."

Turning, Azareela faced me, leaning back against the wall. "I ask you to remain in your room each of the nights that you're here."

I couldn't promise to do that, though I wouldn't try to leave the room again tonight. I sensed she'd be watching, listening. The last thing I needed was to be escorted off the property.

Tomorrow was a whole different ball game.

I strode over to the tray and lifted the cover, releasing a waft of steam. Everything looked familiar but not, and it smelled good.

"Nothing good will come from wandering around at night," she said. "You might . . . bite off more than you're able to swallow."

Fortunately, her voice remained light, and I sensed no threat in her words.

"I recommend you complete your task quickly and leave," she said, crossing the room to smooth the coverlet on the bed. Without glancing my way, she strode to the door, though she didn't open it. "Things will go better for you once you leave the planet."

With a pert nod, she left, locking the door behind her.

I wasn't convinced things would improve once I left. I hadn't been here long, but I already felt entrenched in the mystery surrounding this castle.

Whatever was going on involved Venge—I was certain of that. And I didn't want to leave until I'd found out what.

8

VENGE

I woke hanging from the chains by my wrists but completely myself once again.

The beast had retreated for now. A time would come where that part of me remained forever. I clung to the notion that something would keep it from happening, that I'd be cured and the genetic alteration I was born with would go away forever.

Today, I could look forward to interacting with a highly appealing human female. Why had I tried to drive Jenny away?

In my heart, I knew. I feared she'd discover what I kept hidden, that she'd cringe in horror.

That the mate bond would mean nothing.

Peering around, I was grateful to see I hadn't broken free or harmed someone. Both had only happened once, but I lived in terror it would happen again. After, I'd ensured the chains were more secure and Ressard remained out of my sight after that.

I'd loathed myself ever since it happened.

Once I turned completely and didn't become myself at the dawn of a new day, Ressard would end my existence. In the past, I'd almost welcomed that thought, though I had no interest in ending my life.

"It is over?" Ressard said from the other side of the barred door. Unlike my aunt, he spoke directly to me. He was gentle when he unchained me. "You are yourself again?"

"I am me," I said softly.

With a nod, he unlocked the door and advanced toward me. It didn't take him long to release my restraints.

I sagged against the wall, my arms tingling at my sides. My wrists burned from straining to break free.

"I've prepared a bath in your chamber," he said, turning toward the door. "I thought to include a meal, but the human female is awake and making demands already."

"What kind of demands?" I followed him, grumbling about her impertinence, but secretly smiling. Despite my wish to send her way, I'd enjoyed her spunk. "What does she ask for?"

We strode down the hall and stepped inside the lift that swiftly took us up to the level with my rooms. Her rooms were on the same floor and wing. A mistake on Azareela's part or had she done it on purpose?

"She wishes for bits of what she calls leever," Ressard said with a scowl.

"What is it?"

Ressard shrugged. "She described it as an animal food source. We don't have anything like it here."

"I'll ask her about it."

I could almost taste Ressard's relief. "Very well, thank you."

"Anything else?" Surely asking for leever wasn't enough to agitate Ressard?

"She is also demanding access to your presence."

"Interesting." My heart thudded, picking up speed. She wished to see me? I shouldn't read anything into this. I'd hired her for a job. I must assume she wanted me to give her a timeframe and introduce her to the culairs.

We entered my room, and I quickly removed the scrap of material covering my groin. With a heady sigh, I climbed inside the enormous tub, sinking into the steaming water. My muscles groaned with joy.

Jenny wanted access to my presence, did she?

"Send her to me," I said, my eyelids sliding closed.

"While you bathe, sir?" Ressard asked, his feet shuffling on the wooden floorboards.

"Why not?"

Ressard only grunted.

And as he left the room to retrieve her, I grinned.

9
JENNY

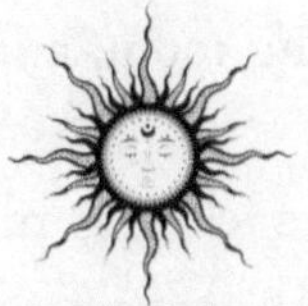

Ressard hurried down the hall, leading me to Venge. When he'd knocked this morning and told me he'd bring a tray to my room for breakfast, I told him I was going to dine with Venge. The staff may not eat with him, but if I hoped to build a bond between him and his pets, I'd need to get to know him better. Meals were a great place to start a friendship.

I didn't want anything else.

My scoff rang out because I couldn't even convince myself about that. I did want to get to know Venge better, though it had nothing to do with my attraction to him. That was caused by hormones and nothing else. I hadn't been with anyone in a while. Thurston, never. I'd kept him at arm's length, insisting I was saving myself for marriage.

My second scoff rang out. I'd only been saving myself from him.

Ressard shot me a look I couldn't decipher.

"What?" I asked, my face overheating.

His eyes darted away from mine. "Nothing."

When we reached the end of the hall and a door, he stiffened. After smoothing his tunic, he looked up at the ceiling as if praying for guidance. With a long exhalation, he opened the door.

I stepped inside the room, and he closed the panel behind me.

The curtains were closed, making it a challenge to see.

"Come closer," Venge said in a deep, seductive voice from the opposite side of the room.

No, wait. He wasn't trying to seduce me. This was his gruff, I-haven't-had-coffee-yet morning voice.

"Are you opposed to light?" I asked, stepping forward. My shoes sunk into the thick carpet, and I nearly ran into an enormous bed before diverting around it.

"What would you like to see?" he asked.

"It might be easier to find you if you turned a light on. And easier to avoid tripping over something." I approached a window draped with heavy fabric. After sweeping it to the side, I turned.

Venge sat in a tub two to three times his size, lounging in steaming water. I doubt he wore a swimsuit, and I was tempted to step forward to find out.

"Do you always invite women into your bedroom when you're taking a bath?" I asked, remaining by the window.

"You said you wished to speak with me."

"When you're clothed."

He huffed. "My time is precious."

"Yet you hired someone to help you tame your pets. That will take time."

"Come closer."

My voice came out breathy, like I'd run a thousand miles. Could he tell he flustered me? "I'm not interested in viewing your cock."

"It's a nice cock," he said with a snort.

"Every guy says that."

"I'm sure they do."

I moved away from the window and sat on the end of the bed facing him. He was only a few feet away, and I could pick up water droplets gleaming on his shoulders. His wet hair hung over the edge, dripping onto the floor. He must've washed it, and I suppressed the urge to creep closer and run my fingers through it.

"What did you wish to speak with me about?" he asked. He lifted a piece of cloth from the water and ran it down his arm. His hand dipped back into the water, moving downward. It wasn't a sensual thing, but my heart pattered, and my body softened like I'd taken a shot of hard liquor. A languid feeling swept through me, and a big part of me told me it would be very easy to remove my clothing and climb into the bath with him. I could wash his chest.

"You are welcome to do it," he said, humor shining in his voice. He held up the cloth, and I watched the water droplets fall, sparking like diamonds in the sunlight streaming through the window.

His tail flipped lazily back and forth, the fluffy tip skimming the air just above the floorboards. What would that feel like gliding across my skin?

"Jenny?" he said in a low voice, then louder. "Jenny?"

I sucked in a breath. "What?"

"Do it if you would like."

Oh, hell, yeah, I wanted to do it.

Hold on. I didn't want to do anything with him.

My face hot, I stiffened my spine. "Do what?"

He chuckled.

I slid off the bed and inched around the room to stand at the bottom of the tub, though avoiding his tail. The fluffy tip kept teasing across my ankles. This is what I got for wearing low-cut socks.

The water was clear. Heavenly clear. And the parts of him he'd clothed yesterday were as tasty appearing as the parts he'd revealed.

I frowned. "You have a tattoo on your chest."

He stroked the image that reminded me a bit of a yin and yang that symbolized the interconnectedness of the world. "It is not a tattoo."

"There's no up without down," I whispered. "No laughter without sadness."

"What do you mean?" he asked, his gaze gliding down my front.

My knees loosened, and in a flash, my panties were soaked. How could he do this to me with one glance?

"Yin-yang," I said, pointing to the mark. "That's the meaning of the symbol."

"Not for my species." His brow narrowed. "You can touch it if you want."

My lips quirked up before I could hold my smile back. "Guys say that all the time too."

"I meant the symbol," he waved to his body in general, "but you are welcome to touch whatever part of me you like."

"I came here to tame your beasts," I said, my feet taking me around the side of the tub. I *did* want to touch the tattoo. Him too. It was crazy. I was here to do a job. I'd be gone within a week. Falling for him would be dangerous.

"Perhaps there is a beast here you are unaware of," he called out. His gaze slid away from mine as I tried to figure out what he meant by the comment.

"Do you growl at night? Bite?" I asked, joking.

His lips curled down, and the silliness left like it was punched from the air. "More than I would like."

Weird. "You're not growling now."

"And that is a good thing." He waved to his chest. "Touch it. You know you want to."

"It's just ink under your skin."

He shook his head. "It is anything but. I told you that you made this symbol appear on my chest?"

"You said that, yes, but it's not possible. There's no way I could do anything like that." I couldn't stop my hand from stretching out, approaching the symbol. I swore tiny flames licked beneath his skin's surface, spiraling around the outer ring before swooping through the lines intersecting the circle.

Stooping lower, I put myself at his eye-level. He had gorgeous eyes, a deep purple that was almost black. I leaned forward, as if getting closer would allow me to see . . . everything. Not the surface; everything he kept hidden inside.

I swallowed; my mouth dry.

When I touched the symbol, the flames I thought I'd imagined flared, sparking across my fingertips.

"It's warm," I said. "Hot."

So was I. Lust swirled through my body, telling me I should strip and climb into the tub with him. No, I'd climb on top of him, centering him at my core.

I swore flames licked up my arm. Heat roared through my chest.

I snatched my hand back, realizing how close I was to him. I'd somehow leaned over the tub.

He lifted my chin, making me meet his eyes.

"Jenny," he groaned. "You are incredibly tempting."

He was my boss. I shouldn't want to devour him.

"Why is the mark hot?" I asked.

"Because it symbolizes us."

"There is no us," I stuttered out.

"Not yet."

"Not ever. I just ran away from a relationship that was no good. I'm not about to jump into another."

His head cocked. "How do you know it would not be good between us?"

I didn't, but I wasn't going to say that; it felt too much like a dare.

He lifted his head off the tub surrounding, moving it closer to mine.

My tongue darted out to glide across my lips, and he watched the movement, his eyelids hooding.

Then he leaned forward and claimed my lips with his own.

I melted against him. I'd been kissed before, plenty of times. But none of the others made fire flutter through my body.

As his tongue parted my lips and plunged into my mouth, I placed my full palm against his tattoo—the one that wasn't exactly a tattoo. Like I'd put my hand on the burner of a stove, my skin seared, though without pain.

I gasped, wrenching my mouth away from his. "I . . . I . . ." Turning my hand, I gazed down at it, expecting to see the symbol cauterized into my palm, but finding only my regular, smooth skin. "What are you doing to me?"

"I could ask you the same thing." His brows drew together. "I should not touch you or be near you."

"Thanks?" What was I supposed to say to something like that?

A shutter went over his face, blocking his emotions from me. "You need to leave."

Here we went again. "I'm staying until I train your pets."

"I meant my room." He gripped the sides of the tub and started to stand.

I spun before I could see—much.

"What are you doing?" I asked, my hands fluttering at my neckline. His kiss was addictive enough. His muscular body coated with water? I couldn't stop thinking about running my hands across the smooth surface, licking the water droplets off his abs.

He was huge in so many ways, especially his cock. It was erect! One kiss, and I'd given him a hard-on. It was all I could do not to spin around and drop down in front of it. I'd take it in my hands, and then into my mouth.

Blue, veiny, and I swore I'd seen small flaps along the sides of the rigid length. What would those do?

It was best not to think about that. I'd never be in a position to find out.

"I have finished my bath," he said with a low laugh. "The water has chilled, and I need to get out."

He was right. I did need to leave.

I rushed to the door and hauled it open.

"I will see you at breakfast," he said softly. "I look forward to it."

I closed the panel behind me and fled down the hall.

10

VENGE

I was a fool for taunting her into touching me. And I was a fool for kissing her.

But I'd been unable to resist. When her fingers traced across my korier symbol, lightning had shot from my chest to my cock. It stiffened immediately. My body demanded I sweep her up, lay her on my bed, and devour her.

Claiming her would be a big mistake even if she welcomed my actions. What would happen when the sun set and my body hardened to stone? I'd morph into a beast in front of her eyes. She'd cry out in horror and run.

I'd give chase, and there was no telling what my beast would do with her when it caught her. Rumors abounded about what happened to prior generations of my family and of those they'd harmed.

There were no stories about those of the third generation who'd stumbled upon their korier mate, however.

All had lived in this gloomy place until they succumbed and were humanely put out of their horrifying existence.

I should make her leave before I did something I'd never be able to live with. Then I could wait for the beast to fully claim me and the release that would follow.

Grumbling with indecision, I dried and dressed quickly, rushing through the halls to the dining room. Despite telling myself I needed to place her in a one-way shuttle that would take her away from me forever, I was unable to resist seeking her out.

The clink of tableware greeted me in the hall outside the dining room. She was inside, eating. I could go to the kitchen and obtain a meal there, then retreat to my rooms, or I could join her.

Driven by something inside me I couldn't define, I stalked into the room.

She stood in front of the meal synthesizer while it hummed, preparing her breakfast. Azareela watched with a beaming smile on her face.

The device dinged and the door swung open, revealing a heaping platter of food.

"See?" Azareela said. "As easy as that."

"This is amazing," Jenny gushed, grinning at Azareela. Jenny reached into the device and lifted out the platter. When she turned, she spied me watching, and her hands trembled, making me worry she'd drop the meal.

I moved forward and took it from her, turning to put it on the table.

Two places had been set close together despite the

table being able to accommodate more. If groups had dined here, it hadn't been when those of the third generation were waiting to change fully. I assumed some who were not as unlucky as us used this castle for vacations, though I couldn't imagine anyone choosing to spend their time here if they didn't have to.

Jenny stared at her place setting for a long time before sitting.

I dropped into the seat beside her, trying to ignore when she shifted her chair away from mine, though grateful that Azareela left the room. She closed the door between the dining room and kitchen, leaving us alone.

"We need to get started with the culairs right after breakfast," Jenny said, her voice all business. "I'll need some sort of treat to offer them. I used bits of liver on Earth, but it doesn't appear you have anything like that here."

"What is this leever?"

"It's organ meat." She tapped her belly. "A liver."

"Ah." I frowned then reached to lift a piece of meat off the platter. "Would this do?"

She took it from me and sniffed it.

I scented her, my eyelids sliding closed. She smelled amazing. If only I could taste her.

The beast inside me huffed and blew, but it was strangely calmed by the light floral essence wafting off her skin. Was it something she wore or pure Jenny?

"That will do," she said decisively.

My eyes opened.

She placed the meat on her plate and added other

food items from the platter. "I don't usually eat a hearty breakfast, but this all looks wonderful."

"It is food," I said dryly. Everything she did disconcerted me. Her sharp wit kept me alert. Her scent made me ache to lick her. And the calm way she treated me made me want to lounge through the day with her draped across my lap and love her all night.

It might be wrong to pursue her, but I couldn't help it.

"Aren't you going to eat?" she asked, waving to my empty plate. She picked up her dining spire and speared a small piece of meat from the platter. "How about this?"

The unruly light in her eyes made me open my mouth, and she fed it to me. I chewed the piece, finding pleasure in this simple action for the first time in forever. For too long, I'd wallowed in what I was about to become, rather than enjoy the fact that I was still myself for now.

Would it be so wrong to snatch a bit of time with Jenny? So far, the beast only took over at night. I could stay away from her during that time.

I walked on shaky ground, but I couldn't help but believe Jenny could keep me stable.

After filling my plate, I picked up my own dining spire and fed her a bite.

She smiled as she took it, chewing. "We really should eat our own meals, don't you think?"

"Why?"

"Because that's how it's done."

"Not here. In this castle, there are no rules."

"Oh, is that right?" she asked with a soft laugh that tickled through my bones. "Maybe that's why you have two unruly culair pups?"

"They get their unruliness all on their own," I said with a chuckle. I liked this female because she was highly attractive and witty. Even if my korier symbol had not flared for her, I'd want her.

"Exactly what are we dealing with here?" she asked. "I didn't get many details before I took the job."

"I think you are the type of person who would thoroughly evaluate a position before accepting it."

"I'd just ditched my ex. I worried he'd catch me and drag me back to marry him."

A growl ripped through me. "He would force you to be with him?"

She leaned back and tilted her right leg my way, revealing a red mark around her ankle. "They kept a zapper locked around my ankle. It tracked my every movement and would deliver . . . punishment if I didn't do as they asked."

"They?"

"My ex, Thurston, and my father."

"Your parent did this to you?" I fumed, my voice lifting.

"They wanted the credits my grandmother left me in a trust."

"And they thought that marrying you to this . . . Thurston would allow them access," I said with a snarl. If they were here, I'd claw them to bits.

"The trust indicates I can access the credits either

when I turn twenty-five or marry. I'm twenty-eight, but my father has prevented me from reaching a facility where I can withdraw the funds and flee. Hence the zapper." Her gaze traveled to my hands clenched on the table, and a frown filled her face. "So tell me . . ."

"What would you like to know?"

She nudged her chin toward my wrist. "Who put a zapper on you?"

11

JENNY

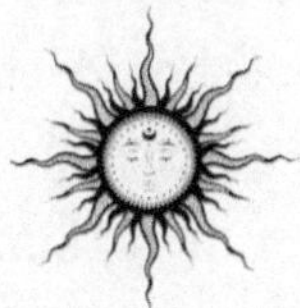

"No one put a zapper on me," he said harshly, dragging his hand off the table and stuffing it down by his side.

"You're burned, then," I said, pain stabbing through my chest. "How did it happen?" A horrifying thought burst through me. I well knew how terrifying it was to have someone hurt you. "Who did it?" I'd kill them. Rip them apart. Toss them off a cliff.

I didn't know this guy well, but I already ached to protect him.

"It is nothing," he snarled, but I was more interested in the pain filling his eyes than the tone I'd already suspected he fell back on to push others away. "Forget you saw it."

"If someone's hurting you, tell me. Is it Ressard?"

"He would not harm me."

"Azareela? There must be other staff here. Tell me who did it."

"No one will touch me until they must," he clipped out, standing. "Are you finished?" Gone was the fun guy I'd fed, the one who'd teased as he tucked bits of food into my mouth.

"I'm finished with the meal, but I'm not finished with this." I pointed to his wrists where the red marks flared, as angry as him. I should let it go. It wasn't any of my business. But I wanted to grab a sword and challenge whoever might've done it to him. Stab them to keep them from doing it again.

He sighed, and his lips thinned. "I'll take you to the culairs." After snagging a few links of meat off the platter and wrapping them in a cloth, he started for the archway leading to the hall. "Come with me. I left them in the living area yesterday, but Ressard always moves them to their outdoor pen at the end of the day. They have a dwelling and food there."

My gaze traveled down his other arm, and I found a matching red ring around his wrist.

"Don't think I won't look into this," I said, my eyes stinging. All I could think of was him being hurt. If I didn't know better, I'd suspect someone bound him. Who'd do such a thing?

He froze in the doorway. "I asked you to let this go."

He couldn't tell me what to do. I'd long since determined if I ever escaped my father and Thurston, no male would ever control me again.

Not even someone as intriguing as Venge.

But for the sake of peace between us, I said nothing. I

followed him down the hall and through so many passages, I lost count.

"Why do you live here?" I asked.

He didn't say a word.

"This place is so stark. Why not live where there's bright light and flowers?"

Still saying nothing, he strode a pace ahead of me, going faster.

"You mentioned family," I said. "Your people. Azareela told me—"

"Azareela should not speak of me or my past," he growled.

"She was just being friendly. She said she wouldn't be able to marry until she returned to your home world."

"Her marriage is the least of my concerns."

It sounded harsh, but I got the feeling he didn't mean it that way.

We reached the end of a third hall, and he nudged open a door. Muted sunlight greeted us, and when I stepped outside, I took in a big gulp of fresh air. Storm clouds chased each other overhead, and the air held a hint of rain. It had been dark and stormy when I arrived yesterday too.

"Is it always so gloomy here?" I asked.

"Most of the time, yes." He crossed an open, stone deck, and started down a long flight of stairs. A narrow bridge arched over the moat that churned with violent water.

"Why do you stay here then?" I asked, trotting behind him.

"I will remain here until I die."

A sense of doom filled me. "That won't be for a long time. You don't seem much older than me."

He stopped on the bridge, gripping the rail tight enough, his claws dug in. "I am about your age, yes." Turning, he strode across the rest of the bridge and out onto the scraggly lawn.

"Why is the grass dead if it rains so much?" I asked.

"Nothing grows well here."

I waved to the endless forest. "Except for the trees."

"Yes, they outlive us all."

There he went with the cryptic statements again.

I grabbed his arm, bringing him to a halt, though I had a feeling he only stopped because he wanted to. He was nearly twice my size. If he wished to keep walking, I wouldn't be able to hold him back.

"Tell me what's going on," I said when he faced me.

"What's going on is you are going to help me with my culairs." He eased around me and continued toward a big pen ahead. A small hut sat in the middle, but I didn't see any creatures.

He stopped when we were at least ten feet away from the fence.

I came to a halt beside him. "Where are they?" I glanced up at him, then followed his hand pointing in the direction of the hut.

Two scaly red creatures the size of full-grown dogs leapt from the opening in the hut.

While I watched in awe, the wingless, dragon-like

pups raced toward us, their spiked tails lifted and their red eyes glowing.

"Aw," I said. "They're gorgeous."

Venge took a step backward as the pups raced closer, their claws digging into the soil in their excitement to reach us. When they got to the fence, they came to a skidding stop, their gazes focused on Venge.

One stretched its neck out. Its mouth opened.

And a blast of fire roared toward Venge.

12

VENGE

I grabbed Jenny and dove to the side, curling around her as I tumbled across the ground. Once on my feet, I set her well away from me.

I'd barely avoided being fried by Fleese, the craftier of my two pets.

"Whoa," Jenny cried, scrambling backward.

"You don't need to be concerned," I said as I rose to my feet and mentally assessed myself for burns.

Her wide eyes met mine. "They're trying to kill us."

"They're trying to kill me. They haven't met you yet, so there's no saying how they'll behave, but so far, they tolerate my staff. They only hate me."

She frowned, looking up at me. "Why do they hate you?"

"I know what you're thinking."

Her hand jerked up to hitch on her hip. "Oh, you do, do you? Tell me, then. What am I thinking?"

"You believe I am cruel to them, that I hurt them, that this is why they wish to harm me."

"Actually, I don't." Fuming, she stomped back in front of me, though wisely, not getting closer to the culairs who paced inside the fence, growling at me. "I might be stupid, but I see you already, Venge. You're not a mean person."

"You do not know what you are talking about."

She came to a stop in front of me. "Maybe I don't, or maybe I do. I'm good with animals, but I'm also a good judge of character. I say it again. You're not a mean person."

I gripped her arms, holding her still. Desperation filled me. There was so much I wanted from this female, things I could never ask her to give. "I could be. Never forget that Jenny. I could be."

She shook her head, her lovely, dark hair swaying along her back. "I don't believe that. We all get mad at one time or another, and we all do things we regret, but I don't think you're capable of being unkind to others."

I put my face down, close to hers. "Trust me. I *could* be." It was all I would say.

Her lips thinned, and she turned to face the pen. "Something is blocking you and the pups from forming a solid relationship."

That was an understatement.

"I'm going to figure it out and make this work."

"I appreciate it."

"First things first." She took the pack with meat from

where I'd tucked it into my right pocket. I struggled to ignore how close her hand came to my cock.

It jutted forward, eager.

Her smile warmed me through. "I, um . . . Yeah." Color filled her face. "We're not going to mention that." With the pack in hand, she slowly moved close to the fence. "Hey little guys. I've got a treat for you." She shot a glance at me over her shoulder, noting I hadn't moved along with her. "Do they have names?"

"Their parents had silly names, Truffle and Poochie."

"Aw, that's cute. I bet you came up with names just as fun for those two."

"Fleese and Gular."

She snorted. "Not as fluffy as their parent's names, but I like them. Which is which?"

"Fleese has a small scar on the top of his snout from where he banged it on a tree not long after I adopted them."

"Okay. Hey, Fleesey! Gular! You two are cute, amazing culairs. We're gonna be best friends." Stopping a few paces away from the fence, she peeled open the cloth, revealing the meat to the pups.

They sat on their haunches and whined.

Jenny shot me a grin. "I think they'd like a taste, don't you?"

All of us would savor a taste, but she didn't mean me.

I held my breath as she crept right up to the fence, sticking her hand between the slats. First, she let them sniff her hand, though I noted it trembled. Then she broke off tiny bits of the meat and gave a bite to each of them. They gobbled it with one swallow and watched her, their tails swishing across the ground.

Of course, they liked her. Who wouldn't?

"I want to go inside the pen with them," she whispered. "Would that be okay?"

"I do not want you harmed." A protective urge clambered inside me, telling me to jerk her back, out of harm's way. Already, the bond between us deepened. She wouldn't understand if I explained, but I knew on my part, it would only grow stronger.

I'd have to make her leave before it was too late.

"I want to work with them a bit before we slowly introduce you." She crept toward the gate.

I followed, my guts in turmoil. I'd fling myself in front of her and take the burn rather than see even one bit of her flesh marred.

The culairs watched me, but they appeared more interested in the cloth package Jenny held. They trotted along the fence beside her, whimpering with eagerness.

I gave her the code to the gate, but when it swung wide enough for her to slip through, I backed away.

Fleese had turned a grim gaze my way. As he puffed his chest, preparing to blast me, I backed up fast, putting a decent distance between us. My body remained poised to plunge back to the fence and leap over it. If he made one threatening move toward Jenny, it was over. I wouldn't harm him, but I would remove her from their presence, and it would be a long time before I allowed her to get close again.

She didn't approach the culairs. They watched as she

strode farther inside the fenced area. She sat on the scraggly grass and stretched her legs out, placing the pouch of food on her lap.

I moved closer to the fence, my heart floundering, my palms sweaty.

The culairs glanced at me, but they were more interested in Jenny. They tiptoed toward her, and I was glad they didn't split like they did when they planned to attack me. That didn't mean they wouldn't lunge toward her, however.

Why had I set this up? I was endangering the female I was already growing fond of. She sparked me like no other had before.

She gave me hope there was some way I could wrangle out a future for us. A foolish thought. I'd join all the others who'd died before me, exterminated once it was clear I would never turn back to my original form.

Fleese paused, his little claws digging into the dry soil. Gular sauntered over to Jenny, stopping when he was a short distance away. His whine rang out, and it was clear his attention was focused more on the food than her. He stopped and sniffed her knee.

If his tail wasn't sweeping back and forth slowly, I'd leap over the fence and shove myself between them. Instead, I dug my claws into the rail and kept my body ready to move.

A hop, and Gular landed in her lap.

She grunted but shot me a grin that melted through me like the sweetest treat. The symbol on my chest burned again as flames licked along the edges.

She offered Gular a bit of the meat on her palm, and he plucked it carefully from her hand. Even from this distance, I could see he took care not to scrape her flesh with his fangs.

When Fleese sprinted over to join his brother, I braced myself again. But as soon as he'd taken his share of the meat, he also clambered up onto her lap.

They settled, gazing up at her with adoration.

13

JENNY

Venge remained on the other side of the fence while I fed the culairs bits of the treat. The longing in his face to join us was a kick in my gut. I couldn't imagine adopting pets I hoped to have a lasting relationship with, only to have them try to harm me.

With care, I stroked their faces and spines, admiring their rubbery skin and tails with pointed tips. They cooed at my touch and nuzzled my hand.

It made no sense. Why not do the same thing with Venge?

"The key to working with animals is training," I said, softly enough not to concern the culairs but loud enough Venge could hear.

"Exercise is a biggie," I said. "Is it possible to put them on leashes and take them out of the pen?"

He grunted. "I have not leashed them." Scorn came through in his voice. "Why would anyone wish to be bound?"

"It's just a thought. If I let them out, will they run or remain with me?"

"They stay with Ressard when he takes them from the pen to the house and back again."

"That's right. You mentioned you've brought them into the house," I said. Interesting. I'd think if they wanted to harm him, he'd keep them penned out back all the time.

"I want them to feel welcome."

And there it was again, the intense longing I'd seen in him earlier, both with the culairs, and strangely enough, with me.

An answering need rose inside me, an ache for something I couldn't define. I'd never felt such a draw to someone before, and I wasn't sure how to handle it. This wasn't a rebound reaction to breaking things off with Thurston because I'd been forced into the relationship. I'd nearly hated him by the time I stood beside him at the altar.

No, what I felt growing inside me for Venge was friendship mixed in with something that made my knees quake and my heart flounder. I wasn't sure I liked the feeling, but I couldn't seem to resist him.

I should find a way because I wasn't going to be here long. And I wasn't sure he wanted any kind of relationship with me. We'd kissed—a searing, amazing kiss that hadn't lasted nearly long enough. But there couldn't be anything more between us.

"I'll take them for long walks," I said, getting back to the training. The culairs had eaten all the meat and seemed content to lay on my legs. My legs were going to sleep, however. These pups were as big as a medium-sized dog. I couldn't imagine how large they'd grow. "If I wear them out, they'll be calmer."

"I'll walk with you."

"That's a good idea. The more they interact with you in a pleasant situation, the easier it will be for you to earn their trust and affection."

"What else do you suggest?" His intent gaze remained on me, and I got the feeling he'd fly over the fence and attack the culair pups if one so much as grazed my skin with its teeth. These babies wouldn't be the first to bite me, and they wouldn't be the last.

"We'll reward good behavior and shun bad." I hurried to explain. "I don't mean punish them, but it's best not to acknowledge bad behavior, like, by turning your back."

"They try to fry me," he said dryly. "One cannot just turn a back to flames."

Good point. "Consistency is another tactic we'll take. We'll set up a schedule with them and stick to it."

"What if these actions don't make a difference?" Even from a distance, I could hear the desperation in his voice.

"I've never failed. Let's see how it goes before evaluating what we'll do if the initial plan doesn't work."

He nodded.

I carefully shifted the pups off my lap and stood slowly, though I was confident by how they'd behaved so far that they wouldn't turn on me. Still, it was never a good idea to completely trust something that could easily be a wild animal. These weren't domestic kittens who couldn't cause damage even if they tried. These beasties had long claws and sharp fangs, let alone the ability to shoot fire. With their size alone, they could knock me over.

Then they could trample me and rip me apart.

A chill rushed through me, but I shrugged it off. I had to trust my instincts in this because they'd never failed me. They told me the pups wouldn't cause me harm.

They rose to their haunches and looked up at me, their tails swooshing along the scraggly grass.

"Would you two like to go for a walk?" I asked them.

As if they understood, they rose to their feet and started trotting toward the gate.

I followed while Venge undid the latch and backed away.

"Don't make any sudden moves, and it might be nice if you led." I glanced toward the woods. "Is there a path we can take, or should we stay near the castle?"

"There is a path." He watched the pups trot along beside me, and the sadness on his face made my heart jerk sideways. If there was anyone deserving of loving pets, it was Venge. He seemed so lonely.

How could I help him other than by working with his pets?

He stayed well ahead of us as he strode across the lawn. As he'd said, the pups remained with me, showing no interest in straying. Imagine if all puppies behaved in this manner. When they were young, they were happy to remain with their owners, but once they got a taste for how much fun it was to run while others chased after them, they did it whenever they could. That was a common problem I had dealt with, dogs who wouldn't come when called, who raced away whenever the owner got near.

Venge entered the woods, remaining ahead of us and out of fire-blast distance. If the pups continued to ignore him, I'd have him slowly drop back. Eventually, that is. I doubted it would happen today. It was important for him to walk with us, like he was part of the pack.

I didn't know much about culairs, however. "Where did you get Fleese and Gular?" I asked.

"From another planet. An orc who manages a new colony has adults. They hatched ten eggs, and they were giving the pups away."

"That's a lot for one litter."

"He was looking into ways of reducing the frequency of the laying. The planet would be overrun if they had a clutch like that every few lunar cycles."

So far, Fleese and Gular were ignoring Venge, skipping along beside me, their tongues lolling like Earth dogs. They watched the forest intently, but so far, I hadn't seen anything of concern, just a few birds darting away and lush vegetation. All that rain paid off here, where trees could suck it down.

"Does this area of the planet have seasons?" I asked, picking up my speed to gain on him by a few feet. I'd do this slowly, watching how the pups behaved. So far, all was good.

"This region sees a lot of rain, not true seasons, though it does get colder in the winter and hotter during the summer lunar cycles. Right now, winter looms."

"Will you live here forever?" I couldn't imagine why. Sure, the castle was nice, but I craved sunshine every now and then to balance the rain.

"I told you. I will live here until I die."

I thought he was joking. Mostly. He'd said it with all seriousness, but how could it be true? "Why? You're not banished here or anything, are you?" It was a wild guess on my part, one I didn't think was true, but it was conversation. I wanted to get to know him better.

"I am, actually."

My steps slowed. The culairs sensed the change in the air and shot Venge dark looks, the spikes on their backs stiffening. But they held back their fire.

"You were banished here?" I gulped out.

"It was my choice to come here, but some might see it as banishment."

"Why?"

"You ask a lot of questions." Pivoting, he kept walking.

I started moving again, hurrying until we were fifteen or so feet behind him.

"I do ask a lot of questions. Is that a bad thing?"

"I guess it depends on why you ask them."

"Because I . . ." How could I say this? Being truthful was important to me. "Because I want to get to know you better."

"To help with the culairs, I assume."

"That's one of the reasons."

His body tensed and he stopped, though he didn't turn. "What are the other reasons?"

"Is it wrong to tell you I'm attracted to you?"

His breath whooshed out. "It is."

"I'm sorry." My stupid eyes stung with tears. "You're my boss. This is a job. I get it."

"It's not that." He started walking again.

The culairs and I did too, moving faster until we were eight feet or so behind him. So far, the pups ignored him. It was a decent start. If they could remain civil with him, we could work on affection after that. How could they miss how nice he was?

"You're not interested in me, then." Why did I feel upset about it? We'd just met. I'd leave in a week or so once the pups loved him, and he had the skills to move forward with them.

"It's not that either."

"Then what is it?" I struggled not to sound like a whiny teenager in the throes of her first crush.

That's what this was. A crush. He was hot enough to burn skin on sight. Who wouldn't be interested?

"I cannot be with anyone," he said.

"Do you love someone else?" That must be it.

"I do not. I never will."

An odd way of phrasing it. "Because you're banished."

"I am banished for the same reason I will never have time to love someone."

"Would you turn around so I can see your face?" I

asked. "I don't understand and speaking to your back isn't the best way to communicate."

"I will not turn. We will continue to walk. But know that my time is limited on this planet. It would be a mistake for you to love me."

That was taking things pretty far. "Who says I could love you?"

He snorted.

"You've got an inflated opinion of yourself, don't you?" I said, irritation blooming inside me. Irritation beat feeling like crying.

"There isn't time for you to love me."

"You're right," I said, my balloon of irritation popping. He meant because I would leave soon. I struggled to keep moving while the rest of my stress fizzled out of me. "I guess it's good that we've got that straight."

"It is," he said softly.

By now, the pups and I were only six or so feet behind him.

"Let's try with you walking beside me," I said.

Pausing, I stroked the pups, giving them plenty of love to show they were good . . . well, they weren't doggies, but good culies, I supposed.

I kept a hand on each of their heads, scratching behind their pointy ears, while Venge stopped and turned to face us.

Stark pain creased his face, though I didn't know why. We'd laid things out and come to an agreement. We wouldn't mean anything to each other because I wouldn't be here long enough to care, and he was doomed to remain here forever for some reason.

He stared at me with more longing than he showed the pups earlier, but I had to be misreading him. He wasn't interested, so he couldn't ache to be with me.

With slow steps, he walked toward us.

A growl rumbled in Fleese's chest, but his spine didn't bristle. Gular's tail swept back and forth in welcome, but he kept an eye on his brother. When Venge was only a few feet in front of me, Gular growled as well.

"That's close enough," I said. I stooped down, placing myself between the pups and Venge. "Maybe get down as well? We need to show them you mean them no harm. Perhaps letting them sniff your hand is all we should push for today."

He dropped to his knees, though that didn't put him at my eye level due to his huge size. He waited until the beasts stopped growling before tentatively stretching out his hand.

Gular appeared to be the friendlier of the two. He stretched out his nose to Venge's hand and huffed on it.

Fleese watched them, his spikes bristling, but he didn't appear poised to attack.

Venge stroked Gular's face, and the pup whined in pleasure. Emboldened, Venge moved to Gular's ears, rustling them gently in the way I'd already learned the pups enjoyed.

"It's working," he said in awe. He gave me the sweetest smile. He might have a gruff, somewhat grumpy exterior, but inside, he was pure mush.

When I smiled, his grin widened, encompassing me in his wonder.

"Thank you," he said softly. "Thank you so much."

My heart twinged, and I felt like something seismic shifted inside me.

Venge *was* dangerous.

I could love him. Easily.

14
VENGE

We returned to the castle, me walking a solid distance ahead of Jenny and the pups. My steps were lighter. Progress was being made with the culairs. I didn't hope they would cuddle with me by the end of the week, but I also didn't worry any longer that they'd try to kill me.

"I'm going to wash up," Jenny said, after we'd left the pups in their pen and entered the castle. "It's only mid-afternoon. Is there a library or room where I can sit and put up my feet?"

"The library is on the second floor, on the left side of the castle if you are facing the front door."

"Any particular room in the hall?" she asked.

"The room takes up the entire wing."

"Whoa," she breathed. "You have a wing full of books?"

"They are not all mine. I am not the first of my family

to remain here until . . ." Until I died, though I hated bringing that up.

"How many others have lived here?"

"This castle has been in my family for longer than anyone remembers. The son of each third generation is sent here. He remains here until his death."

"Is it a kind of keeper position? Are you a guard against . . .? I don't know what, but something dangerous?"

"In a sense." Not truly, but this might be more palatable than stating I'd remain here until I'd fully succumbed to a gargoyle beast rising inside me. That I'd be killed before I went on a rampage.

"Ah, I see," she said. "This is a job for you, then. A lifetime position?"

"Yes, I will fill this role for the rest of my life."

"Did you apply for it or was it demanded of you?"

If nothing else, she was persistent. I could hold out longer than her. Eventually, she'd feel she had the answers she sought, and she'd stop asking.

"Wait." She frowned. "You said you were essentially banished here." Her gaze shot to the window and outside. "It's isolated and rains a lot. I can see why you feel as if you were condemned to remain here, especially if this isn't necessarily a job you applied for but were assigned."

"That is it."

She nodded and started walking across the foyer and toward the staircase. "All right, then. I'll see you at dinner?"

"Only if you wish to finish the meal before sunset."

"Let's do that. Then neither of us have to eat alone." She strode up the stairs but turned after the first flight. "You don't happen to have an elevator here, do you?"

"Unfortunately, no."

"Or a room on a lower floor?"

I liked having her near me, and I preferred the top floor, though I rarely had the chance to sleep in my bed. As the end of my time approached, the beast came for me more often. It would keep doing this until the blurred line between me and him faded. Then, we'd be one. I'd become whatever the beast was.

Nothing of me would remain behind.

I watched until she had entered the hall with our rooms and disappeared from view.

"Nothing good will come from longing for her," Azareela said from behind me.

"Ah, so you speak with me?"

Her lips twitched. "For now. You *are* my nephew. But back to Jenny. You should stay away from her."

"There is no harm in wishing for something I can never have."

She placed a hand on my arm, her claws digging in just enough to give warning. It wasn't a mean gesture; she was my mother's sister and there were few who cared for me more than her. "I don't wish to see you with your heart broken."

"This appeared when I met her," I said, tugging my shirt apart to show her the korier symbol.

She gasped. "How is this possible? As far as I know, none before you have met their fated mate."

I shrugged. "She is mine, and I am hers."

"You don't have time for that. It would be wrong to pursue her."

My heart spiraled, dragging me to the center of the planet with it. "You are correct. It would be wrong, which is why I will stay away from her as much as possible."

"I can see she is interested in you. Has a matching symbol appeared on her flesh?"

"I haven't looked or asked, but I've seen nothing."

"I am not surprised. It is exceedingly rare to form a true mate bond with both of you hosting matching symbols."

"If one appeared, she would feel the burn."

"Let us hope she does not." Her arms went around me. "I am sorry, my beloved nephew. If only there was a way for you to escape this fate."

"Nothing is ever fair in life, is it? This is how it was for my ancestors. This is how it must be for me. I will live with it."

"And die with it." When she leaned back, tears sparkled in her lavender eyes that were only a few shades lighter than mine. "If I could take your place, I would. Know this."

"I would not let you." When I was born, my mother scorned me, horrified about a fate she couldn't control. She set me aside, deciding it was best if I died while young, best if she didn't come to love the adult male who would change into a beast.

Azareela raised me. She loved me when no one else did. She'd volunteered to come here with me, promising she would be by my side until the end.

I took comfort in knowing I wouldn't be completely alone, that someone who loved me would stand with me when I died.

"I'm going to ride," I said.

"Watch out." Fear flitted across her face, and she darted her gaze to the door. "The woods were alive this morning."

"There is not much I fear," I said. I didn't worry about my death. All of us died. The only difference was I knew my ending was near. "The worst that could happen is some creature in the forest ends things for me sooner."

"Do not speak like that," she barked. Her body curled forward. "*Please* do not speak like that. You have now. You have tomorrow. Do not let them go to waste."

With that, she turned on her heel and strode toward the kitchen.

To keep myself from joining Jenny in the library, I strode to my rooms. I remained there until the change was about to take over and Ressard led me down to the bowels of the castle.

15

JENNY

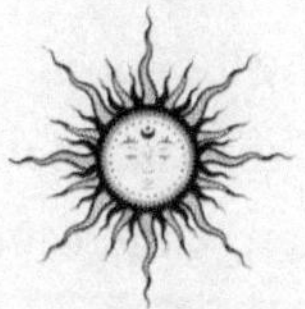

After strolling around and studying the offerings in the library but finding nothing to read in my language, or the universal one now taught to everyone in the Interstellar Alliance, I picked a book with lots of pictures. I settled on a big couch that was more Venge's size than mine and kicked my feet up on the table in front of me.

I lounged in the library for the rest of the afternoon, struggling to read one book after another. There had to be a million of them in the big library. The outer wall of the hallway-long room was made up of windows over-looking the side lawn, but the inner walls contained floor-to-ceiling bookshelves. The top of the room was at least three stories above my head. I could easily picture myself lighting a fire in the big stone fireplace and sipping cocoa on a chilly winter's day. A silly idea since I'd be gone from here within a week or so.

I dropped the latest book I'd attempted to read on the

table, laid my head back on the cushion, and tried to come up with a plan for when I'd leave here. How could I access my credits without my father finding out? He had friends at the bank. Thurston did too. They'd be watching. Perhaps I could hire someone to act as my liaison, someone who could arrange for the transfer of my funds without giving away my location.

Wherever that might be. Maybe there were books here in the universal language that would give me ideas for where I could settle. The colony where the culairs came from could be a likely option. I'd ask Venge about the location later.

Despite him warning me off, I hoped Venge would appear and hang out with me. We could sit close together on the sofa. Maybe share another kiss. I wasn't opposed to doing more, though it was a wild idea to contemplate something like that after our conversation.

I accepted that I was a fool, falling for a guy I couldn't have. There was no harm in dreaming, right? I'd tell no one about my growing feelings.

When Venge didn't show up to brighten my afternoon, I got up and strolled around the enormous room. The long rows of shelves blurred together with nothing to identify them other than the rare spine of a book made of a different color.

Outside, rain drizzled, splatting on the stone windowsills. Clouds rumbled overhead and scurried across the sky like a thick cloak blowing in a gale-force wind.

Partway down the row of books, I found some that

appeared as if they were related to the construction of the castle. Some had pictures. Yay.

Sitting on the floor, I pulled a bunch out and stacked them on the floor beside me. Then I started going through them. I couldn't understand a word of the written portion, but one of the books had a series of interactive pictures that showed the initial construction of the castle in various stages.

From what I could discern, the castle had been a small manor house initially, and subsequent owners had added to it. After a fire—the book showed a gruesome picture of the cratered ruin—someone had begun construction of the huge structure I sat in now. The pictures looked old, though it was hard to tell. But I concluded no one had added on to the castle for many years. From the cracked vids within the pages, I doubted Venge had done more than maintenance on the structure.

An interesting book, but not exactly stimulating. I set it aside.

One of the books in the rest of the pile showed pictures of the castle interior, from small rooms with window seats in the towers to creepy dungeons complete with chains hanging from the wall.

Had many people lived here at one time? I couldn't understand why a sentinel would need to stay in such a huge building. Maybe they got bored and adding to the structure was a way to pass the time. Or they'd mostly been closet architects.

Deciding I wasn't going to discover anything exciting

here, I opted to put the books away. I stooped down to get level with the lower shelf and started stacking them on the wooden surface.

Something glinted deep inside, against the back wall.

Curious, I stuffed my head inside the shelf, trying to figure out why someone would've secured a few pieces of metal to the inside of the bookcase. Hinges?

Hinges suggested a door, though it wouldn't be more than a few inches in height. I couldn't tell from here how long it extended in either direction.

Maybe it was a secret compartment!

I reached—

"Can I help you with something?" Azareela asked from nearby, startling me.

I jerked upward, smacking my head on the top of the shelf. Backing out of the opening, I rubbed the sore spot. "I was just looking at books."

Her gaze spanned the stack I still had to put away. "Those are about the castle. Can you read them?"

I sensed nothing but mild curiosity in her tone. "No, but some have great pictures. They show the history of the building's construction."

"Castle Verlaine has a long history."

"How many years ago was it built?" I sat on the floor, gazing up at her.

"Longer ago than anyone remembers." She glanced toward the entrance of the room. "It will be dark soon. I suggest you return to your room. I'll arrange for a meal to be sent."

"Venge is going to meet me for dinner." And if it

would be dark soon, I was late. Damn rainy days made it hard to tell time.

Her head tilted. "Are you sure?"

I stood, looking up at her. She was a head shorter than Venge, but still towered over me. "He said he would." I trusted his word.

"All right, then. I do believe you should wait in your room until that time, however."

I couldn't see any reason not to go along with that plan. Although, what did she think would happen to me in the library? It wasn't like monsters roamed the corridors of the castle, hunting humans.

At my shrug, she strode across the room with me following. I'd come back after dinner and put the books away—and check out the mystery in the back of the bookcase.

Azareela walked with me to my bedroom door, then waited until I'd stepped inside before leaving.

I was grateful she didn't lock the door and even happier when I spied a steaming bathtub waiting beside one of the windows. The bathroom only contained a weird looking toilet and a sink, and I'd yet to find anything that would substitute for a shower.

After bathing, I dressed in my other outfit—jeans and a tee—realizing I needed to see about fabricating more clothing.

Maybe a dress? It was silly that I wanted to look good for Venge, but I couldn't seem to help it. When he looked at me, I wanted to see approval shining in his eyes.

I sat by the window, watching the lawn and forest,

but soon grew bored. Other than endless rain, nothing happened outside other than a flock of large birds coasting over the forest. They reminded me of vids I'd seen of carrion birds, circling around, seeking something dead or dying to feast on.

With a shiver, I got up and paced the room.

Eventually, darkness took over the world, and no one came to the door to take me down to dinner.

Azareela hadn't come across as disapproving, though I also didn't think she liked the idea of me doing anything personal with Venge. I got the sense she was protecting him, though I had no idea why. He was big enough to watch out for himself.

Leaving the room, I hurried down the endless staircase, rushing into the dining room when I'd reached the first floor. I sat at the table and waited.

Venge did not show up.

Eventually, I synthesized my dinner and ate alone with Azareela shooting me sympathetic looks. Finally, she left the room.

I pushed my food away and got up. Rather than return to my room, I stalked around the castle, but I didn't find Venge. He said he wouldn't be available after dark, but still. He'd said he'd join me, and he didn't come across as someone who didn't keep his word. Not when he'd promised.

Grumbling, I climbed the staircase to my room with Azareela following like a distant shadow.

Before I entered my room, I gave her a raised brow look, but she said nothing, standing near the wall. I didn't need a guard, but it felt stupid to tell her that. With a grumble, I went inside and shut the door firmly.

I stripped and flopped on the bed, staring at the drapes sweeping through the wooden canopy structure overhead. Sleep followed not long after.

Sometime during the night, I woke to cries of pain echoing through the castle, just like the night before. Scooting off the bed, I dressed quickly in the clothing I'd laid across the bottom of the bed and rushed to the window.

But no matter how hard I struggled; I couldn't lift the pane. Had someone locked it? If so, I couldn't find a latch.

With a snarl of frustration, I undressed and climbed back into bed.

Sleep was a long time coming.

16

JENNY

Venge appeared in the breakfast room as I was finishing my meal the next morning, just before I was about to return to the library to satisfy my curiosity about the back of the bookcase.

I was soon distracted by the hurt I felt about him not showing up.

"You blew me off at dinner last night," I said in a low voice, struggling not to give into the sadness consuming me. He looked tired, as if he hadn't slept, and I hated to bring up something insignificant.

"I'm sorry." He sighed. "Something unintended happened, and it kept me away."

I wanted to ask him what it was, but jeez, he didn't owe me an explanation. I was an employee. He was my boss. I was here to do one job only.

"Perhaps another time?" he said.

"All right." I couldn't look at him. Hurt pinched my

heart, and I struggled not to give into it and let it rule the conversation.

Standing, I pressed a smile to my face. Time to put this behind us. He apologized. We were just—sort of —friends.

"If you're ready, we can work with the culairs some more," I said.

"I would like that." His voice came out low and soft, gentle even. A truce, it appeared.

I accepted it, not wanting to wallow in self-pity. It wasn't his fault I liked him more than I should.

We left the building and approached the pen. The culairs heard us and emerged from their hut, rushing toward the fence. They whined, sounding eager.

Venge stopped when we were still some distance from the fence. I took a few steps past him before turning.

"You should walk with me," I said.

"You should work with them first, like yesterday."

"If you want them to come to you, you have to work with them too."

"I understand," he said, scratching the back of his neck. "I'm not afraid of them."

I lifted my eyebrows. "That's good."

"They're smaller than me."

"Size doesn't matter. I was right when I said you wouldn't be mean to others."

A grimness filled his eyes. "And I was right when I told you I could."

"I hope you'll one day tell me why you believe this," I said softly.

He said nothing, just urged me closer to the fence with a wave of his hands.

The pets leapt and squealed as I got closer, tail-wagging happy to see me, and I was grateful for that. It was only a matter of time before they would be happy to see Venge as well. That will be the best day ever.

At least Fleese wasn't growling or glaring at Venge. Gular's tail swept back and forth as he stared at Venge, another good sign.

"What's the code to the gate?" I asked.

"I should program it with your touch," he said, walking up to me carefully. "Then you can come out here to see them whenever you want."

Fleese watched him, but he didn't act aggressive.

Not until Venge had finished with the gate. As it clicked open, Fleese shot fire at Venge.

The quick way Venge reacted showed me this was the norm for Fleese. Venge dove to the side, rolled, and came up to a crouch, watching the culair for another attack.

Fleese whined and watched him, but he didn't give chase along the fence, choosing instead to trot over to where I stood just inside the gate.

It would be a lie to say I was confident being around this culair but backing down would show them I was afraid. Fear was healthy, but we needed to show these creatures they could trust us, not that they could rule us.

I sat and opened the package of meat I'd brought.

Fleese and Gular were soon clambering around me, whimpering and begging for treats.

They took them from me with delicate bites as frustration built within me. I knew it would take time before they'd work with Venge, but I was at a loss. They appeared to enjoy being with everyone but him.

I reminded myself I needed to stick with the plan.

"You have a package of meat you can offer," I said.

"I'll take it back to the castle."

"Why don't you move some distance away and lure Gular to you? We can show Fleese what he's been missing."

"You mean missing out on biting off my hand?" Venge said, and I was glad to hear humor in his voice.

"I don't think he'll do that."

"I'm not so sure."

Venge strode along the fence until he was halfway around the ring before leaping over the top of the barrier. He landed solidly on the ground and sat.

"Gular," he cooed. "Gular!"

Fleese growled but was distracted by the piece of meat I held out to him.

Gular galloped to Venge and nearly bowled him over. He skidded to a stop, sat, and whined for bits of meat.

Venge fed him one bite at a time until the meat was gone. After he'd stuffed the cloth into his pocket, he looked at me for direction. His eyes gleamed with happiness. It warmed me through and gave me hope we could talk Fleese into behaving in the same manner. This wasn't about maintaining my pet whisperer reputation. I wanted to see Venge happy, and it was clear he was eager to enjoy spending time with his pets.

"Try playing with Gular," I said. "Show him you're fun."

"You know I'm not fun," Venge said with a laugh.

"Sure you are. You just haven't let that part of your personality shine."

"I'd like to," he said quietly. "But it might be too late."

"You're not dead, which means it's never too late."

I expected his laugh, not silence filled with sorrow.

Finally, while I dragged a stick along the ground to distract Fleese, Venge spoke. "You're right. It's not too late, is it? For everything."

Did I sense a change in the air? I couldn't be sure.

Gular left Venge and trotted back to us, his spiked tail swaying as it jutted toward the sky.

I played with them both for a time while Venge watched from near the fence. Fleese left him alone. Gular kept approaching him before darting back to me.

As we walked away from the pen at the end of the day, I felt like we'd made progress.

We continued in this manner for the next few days, working with the culairs, though I didn't see any substantial changes with Fleese. Gular had joined Team Venge.

"There's a good boy," Venge said, offering the culair yet another treat. At this rate, they'd weigh a billion pounds by the time I left.

Left.

I didn't like the thought of leaving this place, though

I wouldn't miss the daily rain showers. I liked Venge a lot, and I wanted to know him better.

Time kept slipping away, and I felt like I was about to miss out on something wonderful.

I couldn't grab onto it long enough to make it mine.

17
VENGE

The next day, after another session with the culairs where I made no more progress with Fleese, I decided to take a ride in the forest. Before I met up with Jenny for the early dinner we'd arranged for this evening, I needed to think, something I couldn't do around her *or* the culairs.

I exited the castle and strode to the back pasture, approaching the stables built close to the forest.

My deesure stomped one of his six hooves when he heard me come closer. We didn't keep many deesures here because they needed frequent exercise. Just two. Histane and his mate, Julier.

I swung open the wooden door to Histane's stall and led him out into the open area in the middle of the stable. Julier huffed out her eagerness to run with us. I'd take her on a lead to ensure she didn't wander, though the odds of that were slim. She was carrying young, and he'd watch over her even better than I did Jenny.

This old guy and I had much in common.

I patted his side, and he dropped his head, taking care not to hit me with his horns. I nuzzled his face, grateful for his docile manner. He was nearly twice my size, and there were few foes he couldn't defeat within the forest. The biggest threats rarely ventured into this area.

While I saddled him and then patted his chest, taking care with the sharp edges of his burnished orange scales, his long, spiked tail flicked at insects.

I released Julier from her stall, attaching her long lead to Histane's saddle, then leapt onto the male beast's back. After settling in place, I clicked my tongue, urging him to venture out into the open beyond the stable.

At my guidance, he strode toward the path I'd walked with Jenny days ago. I kept his pace slow until his muscles had warmed, but once we were deep inside the musty forest, I loosened my grip on the reins and gave him his freedom. He broke into a jarring trot that smoothed into a canter, and I rocked easily on his back.

Leaving him to pick our path, I let my brain sink into the dilemma I couldn't shove aside. Jenny consumed my every waking moment, and even at night, when the gargoyle did his best to turn me to solid stone, I still thought about her.

What was I going to do? Time continued to gallop along, taking me with it, and each night took me farther from Jenny.

We weren't making much progress with Fleese, though Gular was turning into a great friend. He came whenever I approached the fence, mewing for treats, and he even snuggled on my lap, though he wouldn't be able to do that for long. He was getting big.

What to do about Fleese, however? I didn't want to split them. They were brothers. Perhaps, if that were the only option, it would be all right to have one pet instead of two. I could find a good home for Fleese or bring him back to the orc breeder and his mate.

This was the practical approach I needed to consider, not a failure. Fleese and I might never get along.

No matter the decision, Jenny's use here was coming to an end. At this point, if she was a regular hire, I could ask her to leave, confident I'd continue to progress, at least with Gular.

The sun's warmth sunk through the leaves overhead, and I savored the rare, nice day since it rained almost all the time. A light, florally scent traveled with us, and the soft crunch of my deesure's hooves on the path was the only sound breaking the silence.

Julier huffed periodically but kept up with us, darting glances into the woods as we crested a small hill and started down the other side.

My heart jolted when a maritrust leapt from the trail in front of us. It lowered its enormous horns and gnashed its fangs. It was rare to see one of these creatures in the woods. They usually avoided coming near the castle. My deesures and I were larger and more dangerous than them.

Two deesures and me? This maritrust must be out of its mind to challenge us.

Histane came to an abrupt stop, Julier almost running into him from behind. Her feet stomped on the trail, and she skittered sideways, nervous.

Why had this one decided to come near?

A cry from behind made my spine tighten.

I turned to find a pack of six maritrust slinking out of the forest, blocking us off from our path back to the castle.

18

JENNY

Before I returned to the library to snoop—if that's what satisfying my curiosity should be called—I looked for Azareela, and found her weeding a front garden I'd missed earlier.

Murky sunshine tried to stab through the gloomy clouds overhead, though without much success. However, even muted sunshine beat rain. I had to wonder how anything grew here with so little light.

Maybe that was why the grass was so scraggly.

I stood beside Azareela while she worked her way along the planter. When she didn't look up, I cleared my throat.

She continued to weed.

Should I find her later? No. I lifted my chin. I had a simple request. It wouldn't take her long to tell me where I could accomplish my task.

Then I could go to the library.

"Can I fabricate some clothing? In particular, I'd love

to make a dress I can wear to dinner," I said as she yanked out what I hoped was a weed. It bloomed, something unusual in this dank, gloomy place.

She carefully lowered the weed into the wooden bucket sitting on the stone deck beside her. "Why would you wish to wear a dress to dinner?"

"Because I want to look nice."

She didn't look up; just kept yanking weeds. At this rate, the long planter spanning the right side of the castle entrance would host nothing but dirt.

"There is no need for you to look nice," she finally said.

"I want to."

"You can't have him," she said. She stopped pulling plants from the box and settled back on her butt, her hands dropping to her thighs. "I do not say this to be unkind. No one can have him."

"That's up to him, don't you think?" I'd never share what he and I'd discussed. That was between us.

"You should leave here," she said with a sigh.

"You're probably right, but I've got a job to do, and I won't leave until it's finished."

She rose to her feet and lifted the bucket. "Then perhaps you should focus on that and not my nephew." Her gaze met mine, and I was surprised to find tears there. "I raised him. I love him. Believe me, there is nothing I would enjoy more than to see him happy. It is not you. It is everyone and him. His fate and the world around us. It controls what is left of his future."

My spine stiffened. "Tell me what's going on."

"I cannot. Sharing information with you or not is Vengestire's decision."

My insatiable curiosity demanded I grab her arms and hold tight until she told me everything, but that would be wrong. So far, he hadn't told me much, and going behind his back was probably the wrong way to go about this.

No matter what, I wanted Venge to be happy.

"I'd still like to fabricate a dress," I said softly. "There's nothing wrong with that."

She inhaled and released another long sigh. "There is so much wrong with everything here, but I will help you with the dress and other clothing."

"Thank you."

She left the bucket, and I followed her inside, where she sanitized her hands at a device inside the small entry. We continued through a series of long halls, eventually stopping at a small room barely bigger than a closet.

A large fabricator, very different from what I used at home, sat on the counter.

Her glance took in my body, sizing me. "What color or design?"

"Something simple. Blue?"

"Length?"

"Above the knee."

She huffed. "Are you sure?"

"You think I shouldn't show off my legs?"

Her brows rose. "Who would see them?"

Venge, but I wouldn't name him. "Me. I'd see."

"You will dine alone. Why does this matter?"

"Venge said he'd eat with me."

Her lips curled down, but instead of anger; sorrow filled her eyes. "You will be hurt, and I do not mean physically."

"He wouldn't do something mean to me. I know this."

"You do not know him at all. You are a kind, sweet female. Under other circumstances, I would gladly welcome you into Vengestire's life. But you encroach on things you do not know, things you will never understand. You must do the job you were hired for and leave as soon as possible."

"I don't think I can do that." Maybe being told I couldn't have him made me want him more.

Or maybe it was Venge himself. He was easy to love.

Love? I scoffed at the idea I could love Venge already, but I couldn't deny the warmth I felt for him growing inside me. It might not be love, but it could be.

"I will not place myself between you and Vengestire," she said. "But I will ask you to remember that he is a good person. His time on this planet is limited."

"He told me he'd be here for the rest of his life. That his job required him to remain here."

After programming the fabricator, she advanced closer to me, stroking my face with her claws. "You are lovely. I can see why he is tempted. But you are right. He will remain here for the rest of his life."

"It's not that horrible a place to live."

Her gruff laugh rang out. "If it was only that simple."

I needed to know the truth about Venge, but how would I find it? "Does he have a fatal disease?"

Her eyes darted away from me. "I told you. I cannot share his secrets."

"I could look for them."

One of her brows shot up. "And betray his trust? If he wants you to know, he will tell you."

I wasn't going to let this go, but there was no reason to tell her my plans. "You don't need to worry about him. He's a grown male. Let him make his own decisions."

"Some tragedy cannot be avoided."

Cryptic, but pressing her would yield nothing.

I tightened my spine. "This is between me and Venge."

"You are correct but know one thing." She clenched her fists at her sides. "If you hurt him, you will face me."

Anger rose inside me. "Don't threaten me."

"Who else but—"

The thunder of hooves outside made her frown. She rushed to the door at the back of the building and swung it open, gasping as two enormous, six-legged beasts raced across the lawn, heading for a large building tucked into the woods on the back side of the property.

"What are they?" I asked as they slowed and trotted into the building.

"Histane and Julier, two deesure Vengestire keeps here for riding in the woods."

"Did they get out? They had no rider."

She shot me a worried look. "Vengestire rode Histane into the forest with Julier following."

He was in trouble. I knew it. Grabbing a stick off the ground, I raced to the section of woods where the two beasts had emerged, ignoring Azareela's shouts that she would get Ressard to go after Venge.

I soon found a trail that looked like it had been trodden recently and ran down it, crying out Venge's name.

19
VENGE

I'd trained for battle throughout my life, but even a hardened warrior would be foolish to take on seven maritrusts at once.

I raced into the woods at my side, hoping to get around the six on the backtrail.

They crashed through the brush behind me, their hooves gouging the soil, their horns slashing and slicing brush. They'd slice *me* if they caught me.

My heart roared up into my throat, and I realized how stupid I'd been to go for a ride without taking weapons. All I had were my claws and tail—the latter more for adornment than anything else. I could wrap it around a creature's neck and tighten to strangle, but that took time, and any creature would fight while I did it.

They raced around me, flanking me, yipping, and crying out in excitement. If a few got ahead of me, they'd move in, tightening a noose around me I'd be hard pressed to escape.

I'd thought I'd die when the beast took over my mind completely. I'd never dreamed my life would end in the woods, beneath the horns, hooves, and fangs of a maritrust pack.

Despite accepting my quickly approaching death, I didn't want my life to be over.

It had so much more to do. I wanted . . .

Jenny.

Her beauty caught my eye. Her humor made my heart lighten. And her sharp wit kept me eager to match it.

I ached to possess her, something I knew in my heart I must deny.

I ran harder, faster, leaping over downed trees and bushes, keeping the maritrust at my sides, preventing them from getting ahead. Thinking of Jenny gave me strength.

I'd get out of this situation, then I'd think about how I wished to spend my final days. I could mourn each passing moment, waiting for the knife to fall, or I could live for now.

Funny how decisions could be made when a person walked along the edge of a cliff with drop-offs on either side. No matter which way I fell, I would die. But ahead . . . Oh, yes, ahead.

Something wonderful waited.

A cry from my right made me falter because it hadn't been made by a beast or a creature of the woods.

I had sounded human . . .

"Venge?" Jenny cried in a fear-filled voice. "Where are you?"

Fuck.

Swallowing hard, I turned in that direction, hoping I'd find nothing waiting on the path but knowing in my heart who had ventured into the woods.

The maritrust were cunning. Two broke off from the pack and veered in the direction of the call, while the others slashed their horns and raced toward me. They'd get ahead of me, take me down quickly, then they'd move en masse toward her. They'd reach her, and I wouldn't be there to protect her.

I burst out onto the path and ran toward where I'd heard her call. Four maritrust drummed the soil with their hooves behind me. I didn't see the other three, but I could hear them scampering through the woods on my left and right.

They were ahead of me and aiming for Jenny.

I pushed myself harder, determined to reach her before they did. What I'd do then, I didn't know, but I would defend my mate to my dying day.

Rounding a corner, I spied her standing still, her eyes wide with terror.

The three maritrusts had found her. She swung a big stick, spinning, while they tried to dart in and impale her with their horns. If they knocked her down, it would be over.

I roared out my rage, and a bit of the gargoyle trapped inside me came through in my voice.

The maritrusts paused and looked toward me. One

darted into the woods, but the others remained, as well as the four still following me.

I leapt and landed beside Jenny.

"Venge. Watch out," she cried, poking a maritrust in the head with her stick.

Snarling, I slashed out with my claws, hitting the beast in the neck. My claws sunk deeply, and the maritrust roared. It whirled around and slammed down the path, smacking into the four who'd followed me. Two turned and raced after the one I'd cut, leaving the one still trying to get to Jenny, plus two others.

Three against me was a much better number.

I growled and leapt onto the closest maritrust, dragging it to the ground. My arms solidified to flexible stone, much like they did at night, and for one moment, I worried this was it, that I'd continue to change and never return to myself again.

That I'd harm Jenny.

But I maintained my wits. *I* controlled my body. That reassured me.

I smacked the downed maritrust with a stone fist, stunning it, then jumped to my feet as the final two raced toward me.

With a snarl, I darted at them, meeting them partway. My fists swung out, hitting each in the face. One dropped to its knees before scrambling to its hooves and fleeing in the opposite direction. The other slammed onto its side on the trail and didn't move again.

I spun to find the first still unconscious on the ground.

Quiet ruled the forest.

Looking down, I watched my arm as the stone merged with my regular blue flesh, leaving me as I was before.

Or was I?

I didn't know what to make of this. There was so little information about how this process went, though I'd been keeping a log for whoever moved into the castle next. My sister had mated and already had a son. In a few generations, others would follow, because that was how it had always been.

My poor great-great nephew would one day take my place here on this wretched planet.

"That was . . . That was . . ." Jenny's terror-filled gaze met mine. "What are they?"

"Maritrusts. They hunt in packs."

"They were hunting us."

"They came after me first, unseating me from my mount. They chased me through the woods until they heard your cry."

Her fingers pressed against her mouth. "I'm sorry. When the creatures raced from the woods and Azareela told me you'd been riding them, I was worried."

"You should not worry about me!" At my roar, the remaining maritrusts scrambled to their hooves and took off, bolting into the forest.

"Don't you know?" Her head tilted. "I can't help it. I keep telling myself I need to stay away from you. That I should focus on the job. But I can't seem to do it. I want to be with you, Venge, even if that isn't forever."

"You cannot. It is not possible." I stomped past Jenny.

She hurried behind me on the trail, catching up to jog beside me. "I'm apologizing again. You're right. But . . . Is it so wrong to want you?"

Pain exploded in my chest. It wasn't wrong, not for someone who had a future.

I sighed. No one could predict how long they'd live. Any of us could die in a moment. Each lived as if they had forever because they felt that way.

I knew my time was limited, but it wasn't over yet.

I could fight this, keep the gargoyle trapped inside me from taking over for as long as I could.

Then I could be with Jenny.

"I cannot offer you more than today. Tomorrow. One day at a time," I growled.

She grabbed my arm, holding tight. "Maybe that's enough."

I told myself to push her away before it was too late, but I realized it already was. The moment the symbol etched itself on my flesh, it was over.

I was hers, and I might be damned for believing in it, but she was mine.

Stopping on the path, I pulled her into my arms. My mouth descended, claiming hers in a kiss that wasn't soft or gentle, though my feelings seared through it.

I wanted this female, and nothing was going to stop me from claiming her.

20

JENNY

"You, *mate*," he said, cupping my face carefully with his clawed fingers. "Are the most precious thing to me. I would kill for you."

"I hope it never comes to that," I said, my heart soaring. I didn't know where this was going, but I would let it sweep me up and carry me along with it.

"I would *die* for you too."

"No." I placed a finger on his lips, which he kissed. "Never say that."

"It is true, Jenny. There is nothing I would not do. I would give the world to you if I could," he said hoarsely, his deep lavender gaze locked on mine.

"I don't want the world. I only want you."

"You have me."

Lifting me off my feet, he raced down the trail. But rather than continue from the woods and into the castle, he deviated to the right, taking a narrow, winding trail that seemed to go nowhere.

It exited in a tiny meadow with a grassy knoll covered in pale purple blossoms.

"It rains here all the time," I said in awe. "How is it possible for anything to grow?"

"There is sunlight, like today, though it is rare." He paused in the middle of the meadow. "Because we see it so infrequently, it is all the more precious." He lowered me to my feet. "Like these flowers that only bloom in the sunlight. And you."

I wanted so much. My heart was bursting with emotion. But I hadn't known him long. I didn't worry I was jumping into something too fast, but I did worry he'd suddenly change his mind and no longer want me.

"I will not push you," he said solemnly. "We have time."

I looked up at him, trying to read the emotions in his face, but I sensed only sorrow. "How much time?"

"At best, a lunar cycle."

Only a month? What was going on here, and why wouldn't he explain? I wanted to beg him to explain, but I didn't want to ruin this moment. It was special.

I dropped down onto the flowers, hating that some got crushed, and lay on my back.

He smiled at seeing me splayed out before him. In seconds, he was on his knees, straddling me. He braced himself over me and leisurely kissed me. His kiss might be smooth and undemanding, but it lit a fire inside me I believed would never go out.

A month with him would never be enough, but no time at all with him would be worse.

Perhaps I needed to savor now and not worry about tomorrow.

He kept kissing me, his tongue teasing across mine. His fingers glided along my shoulder, and I sensed he wanted to touch me in more intimate places, but he was holding back, waiting for my cue.

I arched my spine and moaned, because, really, I'd almost die to feel his hands on my breasts.

With a groan, he lay down beside me, pressing his full length along mine. I turned toward him and kissed him, loving the feel of his fangs pressing against my mouth. I traced my tongue across one, and he groaned. His tail coiled around my leg, the fluffy tip teasing the skin exposed at the back of my waist.

We kissed for a while, me stroking his shoulders and chest, his fingers trailing down my spine and cupping my bottom. He tugged me fully against him, pressing his thick, long length against me.

By then, I writhed in excitement and anticipation. I wanted more, but how did I tell him?

Bursting away from him, I panted. His gaze was focused on my mouth, and while our eyes remained locked together, he moved his fingers from my back and around to my front to tease across my belly. He paused before sliding them up beneath my shirt, and I nodded.

"Yes," I added, as if a nod wouldn't be enough. If he didn't touch my breasts, I was going to come apart. No one would find enough of me to put me back together.

Watching my face, he slid his clawed fingers across one nipple.

A groan was wrenched from deep inside me.

His smile grew. "You're so responsive."

"Touch me."

He tugged up my shirt, helping me take it off. My bra followed, and he eased me onto my back.

Leaning over me, he grazed his fangs across the tops of my breasts. "Jenny. There's nothing I want more than to bring you pleasure."

I wanted to strip off my clothing to give him complete access to everything.

"Do it," I said, half in a dare. How far would he take this?

He cupped my breast and ran a finger across my nipple. At my groan, he kissed his way down to it and sucked it into his mouth.

Heat coiled in my belly and shot downward, making my clit throb. This guy knew what he was doing. When he looked up at me, a hint of vulnerability shone through the lust on his face.

Maybe he wasn't as experienced as I'd guessed. Desire could drive skill.

The feeling was echoed inside me. This was new and wonderful. Special. It could lead almost anywhere, and as much as I wanted to focus on was this moment, I couldn't ignore the pinch of my heart or the hope there could be more between us.

"I'm yours, Venge," I said, holding nothing back. He might reject me later, but for now, I didn't want any confusion between us.

A growl ripped through him, and I felt it in the movement of his mouth on my breast.

Heat continued to roar through me, centering between my legs. It blossomed inside me, spreading warmth, hope, and a feeling I wasn't sure I was ready to face.

"This feels good?" he asked, looking up at me.

"It's amazing. Don't stop."

His smile met mine, his fangs giving him a devilish appearance.

I realized I'd give almost anything to see him happy like this all the time.

"I don't plan to stop, mate," he said.

The term made my heart skip. I was well aware of why some aliens called women "mate." Every time he said it, I felt like he stroked me on the insides.

Did he think there was a bond growing between us?

He flicked his tongue across my nipple, grinning when I gasped. I thrust my chest upward, whimpers of pleasure spilling from my lips.

He teased the nipple between his fingers, taking care with his claws, watching every expression cross my face. I squirmed, savoring this but wanting so much more. Was it wrong to offer myself fully to him so soon? Who the hell knew? All I could do was ride out this moment and see where it took me.

Emotions I couldn't define roared through me. I'd never felt this way for anyone, and I'd be wrong not to feel a bit of fear mixed in with my lust. The more open you were to someone, the easier it would be for them to hurt you.

While his fingers continued to stroke one nipple, he skimmed his tongue across the other. His tail slid along my belly, making my skin quiver.

If he kept this up, I was going to explode, and the impact would be bigger than a supernova.

His tail stroked across my nipple, the tip fluttering. A heady feeling filled me, and I pumped my hips up, seeking something I couldn't define.

I wrenched at my pants, but with heat pouring through me, I couldn't figure out the fastening.

His fingers shifted my hand away and with a twist, he undid the top button.

I shimmied out of my pants, kicking them to the side.

"You are lovely," he said, his heavy gaze gliding down my body. "A gift."

"Then open your present," I said with a smile.

His low chuckle rang out. "Oh, I intend to."

"I want this," I said, needing to make things clear. "I want you."

"For now, I'm only going to touch you."

"I guess that's the point." I'd welcome anything he offered, and my streak of curiosity told me to undo his pants to see what he hid beneath the fabric, but I also didn't want to rush this.

It was important to savor every moment.

He kissed his way down my body then parted my thighs to kneel between them. With care, he lifted each of my legs to rest on his shoulders.

"Everything about you is lovely, mate," he growled. "I can't resist tasting you."

Who was I to hold him back? I had some tasting I wanted to do myself—later.

His fingers coasted down between my wet folds. I dripped for him already.

While his tail moved across my nipples, keeping them at hard peaks, he lowered his mouth to my clit. He sucked it into his mouth and stroked his tongue across it.

My hips jerked up, and a moan ripped from my throat.

His tail left my nipples, stroking down my body to join his mouth between my legs. The tip was fluffy. I wasn't sure what it could do down there, but I was more than eager to find out.

When something soft yet firm poked between my folds, I groaned. His tongue continued to play with my clit, his fangs grazing periodically. Each stroke made fire shoot through me, and I wasn't sure how much more I could take before I shattered.

I rocked up against him, craving everything he had to offer.

Something soft pushed inside me. It was too firm for his tail, but what else could it be?

My shocked gaze met his, and he released my clit. It throbbed, complaining about the sudden lack of attention.

"Do you like the feel of my tail?" he asked, pushing it farther inside me. It paused while he waited for my answer.

"It feels wonderful," I gulped out. I hadn't heard of tail sex, but if Venge was in charge, I was all in.

"Perfect." He sucked my clit into his mouth again and rolled it.

His tail pushed inside deeper then began to move, the soft fluff stroking my inner walls while the firmness inside maintained its stability. It wasn't a cock, but with my eyes rolling back in my head at the amazing sensation, I'd be the last to complain.

"You're very good at this," I gasped as his tail began to move faster. As it flowed, the soft hairs teased. I swore some of them coiled around my G-spot, and that made heady shrieks erupt from my throat. The combination of his fucking tail and his mouth sucking on my clit was almost too much. I couldn't imagine how wonderful it would feel when he fully took me.

And he would. I was determined to claim all of him. He wasn't calling me mate for nothing. I felt the same.

Mate.

It epitomized the feelings flaring inside me.

"Come for me," he growled, only leaving my clit long enough to bark out the words. He ran the soft length of his fangs across it, jerking his head back and forth.

His tail continued to pump into me, going faster.

I bucked against him, my legs splayed wide, my body fully exposed to his touch. I couldn't get enough, but I could feel my body tightening, my orgasm beginning to consume me.

It felt so good, I couldn't keep my eyes open. With them closed, I could drink in each sensation.

"Venge," I cried as the explosion built inside me. My body tightened further as the spasms crested, tugging me along with them toward complete satisfaction.

"Yes, mate?" He made his tail go faster, each drive hitting deep within me. He added a finger, aiming for my G-spot.

My moans echoed through the meadow. I jerked my hips up, meeting each thrust of his tail, and held on to his shoulders. I was adrift during a storm at sea. Each time I rose to the peak of a wave, I shot down the other side. Only Venge kept me from floundering. The feel of his tail moving inside me. The stroke of his tongue on my clit.

"I want all of you," I cried out.

"Soon, mate. Soon. I won't hold anything back." He licked around where his tail still fucked me. "You're so sweet. The best taste in the world. I need more. Come for me so I can savor that flavor as well."

There was no holding me back. Like that raft lost at sea, I could do nothing but hold on, trusting Venge to keep me safe.

"Don't stop," I cried out as the pleasure rose inside me, an inferno only he could extinguish. A few more pumps of his tail, and it would be over.

A new beginning, one that I'd begun to hope would last a lifetime.

"Let go, Jenny," he said. "Give me everything you've got. I'm going to feel you come apart and taste it on my tongue."

I moaned and bucked as a rip-roaring orgasm built inside me. There was no slowing this down. I was going to splinter into a billion pieces and fall back in Venge's arms.

And just like that, he carried me over to the other side. My body shuddered while his tail and mouth continued to pleasure my flesh. I pulsed inside, my body sucking on his tail.

His groan joined in with my cry of bliss.

He tugged out his tail and drove his tongue deep inside me. He licked and sucked while my body gave way again, cresting the peak and falling down the other side.

"Venge, Venge, Venge," I chanted while my insides continued to quiver. I was a limp wreck, and he was to blame.

He lifted his head and grinned. "Yes, Jenny?"

"When can we do that again?"

"You want more?" he asked, his eyes gleaming. "If I was insecure, I'd worry I hadn't satisfied you completely."

Something very hard pressed against my lower leg, about where I'd find his groin if I went seeking.

"Take me," I said, spreading my legs wider.

"Not here." He rose over me and tugged me to my feet, then gently helped me dress.

I wanted to lounge in the flowers while he drove his cock deep inside me, but it appeared he had a different plan. Since I was willing to journey wherever he wanted to take me, I let him lead.

He swept me up in his arms and strode down the trail.

"I can walk," I said in a heady voice. "I think."

"Your legs tremble."

"I just had an amazing orgasm. All of me is trembling."

He continued through the forest, and light bloomed ahead, telling me we'd almost reached the edge.

His low chuckle echoed around us. "You're going to have many more orgasms today, mate."

"Mate." I waited to see what he'd say about the term.

"Is it wrong to claim you?" Pure vulnerability came through in his voice.

"Nope," I said, tightening my arms around his shoulders. "I feel the same."

"Jenny." My name came from his lips like a prayer. He kissed me swiftly before breaking into a jog, carrying us from the forest and across the open, coarse field behind the castle.

Inside, he entered a hall that ended at a second staircase at the back of the castle I hadn't yet discovered. As if he did this all the time, he carried me up the same number of flights I took each day.

"We're going to my room?" I asked, clinging to his shoulders.

"My rooms are near yours."

Of course they were. I'd wondered why he put me at the top of the castle. He hadn't known me, but maybe right from the start, he'd wanted me near his rooms.

A kick of his foot, and his door swung inward, revealing a suite twice the size of mine. I couldn't complain; my room was twice the size of my nice apartment back on Earth.

With the door shut behind him, he strode to the bed and laid me on the soft, velvety blanket.

I scooted to the edge, not wanting to remain dressed any longer than I had to. He felt the same, nearly ripping his clothing in his haste to get naked.

This was it. We were going to do it. Would there be a way to go backward from here?

I didn't want to. I was completely his for as long as he wanted me. I'd never felt this way about anyone, and I wanted to drink in the heady feeling for as long as I could.

Because Venge said his time was nearly over.

21

VENGE

My need was insatiable, my cock a thick rod slamming against the inside of my pants.

Feeling her fall apart . . .

Tasting her pleasure as she erupted . . .

There wasn't anything better than that.

And she'd called me mate. Somehow, deep inside, she knew we were meant for each other.

We didn't have much time, but I was determined to love her as completely as I could before it ended.

Shakes racked my frame, and I swore my skin hardened, flashing from the gargoyle who ruled my nights, then back to me. I must maintain control. Hurting her was the last thing I ever wanted to do.

She was the loveliest being I'd ever seen, a petite frame made up of lush, smooth skin, curves I ached to sink my finger into, glorious hair I'd tease across my skin as soon as I could, and fingers that would soon drive me to the edge.

I'd plunge over the side, taking her with me.

Her heart shone on her face, or so I told myself. It hadn't been hard to fall in love with this female. While I ached to ask if she felt the same, I would save that for later. Now was the time for me to give into my carnal needs while bringing her pleasure again.

I stalked toward her, my cock fully erect, a pole jutting against my abdomen. "You are mine."

She watched me approach her, her tongue gliding across her lower lip. "I'll never belong to anyone else."

That kicked me in the chest, because I hated having no control over my future, that soon, I'd be forced to leave her. I didn't want her mourning or remaining alone when I was gone. She was a vibrant woman, and she deserved so much more than to long for me.

My heart surged to hear her words, however, and the beast flickering to life inside me shouted approval.

I backed her against the wall, then lifted her up so I could find her mouth with mine. My tongue plunged inside her, shouting my need.

Whimpering with pleasure, she wrapped her legs around me, but with our heads even, our height differences wouldn't let me drive myself inside her. She stroked my back and writhed against me, rubbing her clit against my torso.

My skin flexed, and my cock grew more rigid, something I didn't believe was possible. It felt fused with the gargoyle lurking inside me, turned to stone. Claimed like the rest of me would be one day.

She continued to grind against me, the moans in her throat growing urgent.

I pivoted, and holding her against my body, took her to the bed. She was tiny in comparison to my bed, but it was built for my frame. I unwound her arms from around my neck. Her legs remained locked on my torso.

"No," she cried, thrashing her head. "So close."

"I'll take you all the way, mate. I promise."

At my urging, she released me, dropping her feet to the floor. I turned her and laid her across the edge of my bed. Her feet didn't touch the floor, but the height was perfect for me.

I moved behind her, spreading her legs with my knee. She was so tiny. Tight even to my tail.

Would my cock engorged with my gargoyle beast fit inside her?

I stroked down her wet slit, moving my finger lower to find her clit. While she bucked back against my fingers, I inserted a knuckle inside her. Claws would never do.

She dripped for me.

My groan filled the room. "Mate."

"Take me. Please," she whimpered. "I need it."

"I will give you all I can." That was the most I could promise. If she couldn't take my length, surely, she could take the tip. That would be enough for both of us.

Leaning over her, I fondled her breasts, teasing her nipples until they formed ripe buds.

She pressed back against my stone length, spreading

her legs wider. Her whimpers joined with my groans, and I truly felt I'd spill my seed on top of her, rather than inside her.

"Now, Venge. Now!" she said.

I centered my cock at her core and tested, pushing the head between her folds.

She moaned. "Good. Good. Don't stop!"

Her incredibly tight body encased me, and, when I pulled back and inserted the head again, I couldn't get over the sucking sensation of her wet sheath. I was going to explode. Who needed to be buried all the way to the hilt?

I pushed forward again, inserting a bit more of my cock. I couldn't deny it. The gargoyle part of me had claimed that part of me. I'd never been so rigid, so filled with blood and stone. If I wasn't careful, I was going to rip her apart.

"Burns," she shouted, her head thrashing. "It burns."

I wrenched backward, pulling out of her.

"No . . ." she cried. "Give it back to me. I need it."

"I'm hurting you," I growled, nearly overcome by the beast for the first time other than at night. I walked a fine line with him on one side, me the other. Only a thin wall kept us apart, and I'd maintain it to my dying day.

Ironic, since the day it and I fully merged would be the day I'd die.

"It doesn't hurt," she said, her face pressed against my covers. "It feels so good. I want to feel all of it. I'm greedy, Venge. Give it all to me now."

I chuckled, and despite the urge to do as she commanded, I held myself back, slowly pushing my thick cock into her lush body. She was incredibly snug. There was no way the entire length of the fence post between my legs was going to fit inside her.

"More, Venge. More."

I couldn't help it, damn me.

I pulled back, then drove myself all the way to the hilt.

Waiting, I expected her to cry out in pain. To struggle and beg for me to release her.

Instead, she pressed back. "Move, damn you."

My laugher rippled from deep inside me, and for one second, I swore the gargoyle's voice combined with mine. It didn't matter. I was in control, and my mate enjoyed having my cock deep within her.

I pulled out and pushed back inside, nearly going out of my mind at the wonderful feel of her wet body accepting me. Sucking on my cock like I hoped her mouth would one day do as well.

"Fast," she commanded.

Who was I to deny her? She was my everything, my sole reason for existing. This moment and this female were all I needed.

As a test, I pumped my hips back and forth, sliding out of her before shoving myself back in. I remained tense, awaiting her cry of pain.

Her moans of pleasure echoed in the room. She moved, pushing back when I drove forward, our bodies a melody only heard once in a lifetime.

With a shudder, I was overcome. While I struggled to remain in control, the beast urged me on, telling me to fuck her hard, to take all she had to give and more.

I succumbed, but only to the driving need that fused with mine. I'd never let the gargoyle take charge. But in this, we were in complete agreement.

Holding her hips to keep her from being driven forward, I moved faster, pummeling her body with mine while her whimpers of joy filled the room.

"Yes," she kept shouting. "More!"

It was too much and not enough. My body tightened. My balls overheated. And my cock grew more rigid, turning completely to stone.

"Ahh," she cried. "Yes."

I nudged my tail beneath her, seeking her clit. And when the firmness within the soft stroked her, she gave way. Her body tightened around mine, then quivered as her orgasm grabbed onto her and shook her.

With a grunt, I pushed harder, riding her while she crested one surge after another. Only when she collapsed, fully spent, did I shoot my seed deep within her. It was a stupid, silly thing, my seed.

But it was all I could give her.

I collapsed on top of her, though I braced myself, fearing I'd crush her.

Her body shook, and for one moment, I thought she trembled with fear.

"That was amazing," she said, her voice muffled against the covers. "You're definitely going to have to do that again."

"Mate," I said, coiling myself around her.

With awkward movements, I brought us up onto the bed. I'd locked inside her, and my cock would not release for a bit of time, but that didn't mean I couldn't hold her.

"You feel thicker," she said.

"I've knotted within you."

"It feels wonderful." She rubbed her face against my arm.

Her body stilled and her fingers traced along my arm, stroking. "Your skin. It's hard, like you're turning to stone."

A shudder ripped through me as the horror sunk deep. I tensed, waiting for her rejection.

"I like it," she said. "It feels great."

"What?" I barked hard enough even my cock jerked inside her from the movement.

"I love how hard you feel. It's like your entire body is erect solely for me. It's incredibly sexy."

She wasn't revolted at the bit of gargoyle seeping through to claim me?

This wasn't possible. No one cherished the beast, not even me.

"I swear your cock got hard like this when you were inside me," she said.

I waited for condemnation for this, because no one would welcome a stone cock surging inside them.

"That felt wonderful too. Once you've unknotted, I want to feel it again."

"Mate." I couldn't get out anything but that one

word that meant so much, it encompassed the world. "Mate."

For the first time since I was banished by my family, my eyes burned with tears.

22

JENNY

I woke at sundown, alone in a chilly bed.

"Venge?" I whispered, sitting up, holding the blankets against my chest to keep them from falling and exposing my naked body.

If I didn't have a subtle, somewhat pleasant burn between my legs, I'd think I'd dreamed what happened.

Of course, I'd have to sleepwalk, too, since I wasn't in my own room.

I lifted my voice. "Venge?"

When he didn't reply, I tossed back the covers and slid off the bed. I dressed fast in my clothing, tiptoeing around to collect the items off the floor.

After searching his rooms and not finding him, I left. He wasn't in the hall, and despite searching the areas of the castle where I'd already ventured, I didn't find him.

I did find something odd, though. In a room off the right hall on the second floor, as I hurried through it to the room beyond, my shoulder brushed against a drape I assumed covered a window. But when the drape caught on my arm, it was tugged to the side, revealing writing.

Pausing, I turned, my head tilting. "What's that?" I whispered.

Creeping back to it, I assumed I wouldn't be able to read the writing. Everything else in this place was written in a foreign language and not in universal.

I tugged the drape completely to the side, revealing a list of . . . names?

"Okay, so, that's not exactly weird." I'd started to cover it back up with the cloth when I found Venge's name at the bottom. The bright gleam of it suggested it had been etched into the list recently.

I shook my head slowly, unsure what to make of this. With a shrug, I decided to go to the library and check out the bottom bookshelf.

It didn't take me long to remove the books from the shelf where I thought I'd seen the hinges, but when I tucked my head into the hole, I found a smooth wooden wall, as if there had never been hinges or a hint to a secret compartment.

Weird.

Had I imagined I saw something here? I ran my fingers along the surface, but I didn't feel anything unusual.

I rocked back on my heels and shoved my hair off my face.

"I could've sworn I saw something."

With a grunt, I returned the books to the shelf, inched forward along the wooden floorboards, and started tugging out random books, looking for what I'd seen before.

I continued forward, pulling books out at intervals, stuffing my hand between the tomes to feel the back wall.

About ten feet or so from where I thought I'd seen the hinges, I felt something in the back of the bookcase.

With excitement coursing through my veins, I removed a large section of books, enough that I could shove my head into the opening to check it out.

Ah, ha.

Just like I'd seen the other day, I found metal hinges. I traced my fingers along what felt like a small door about a foot long and maybe eight inches high. The edges felt rough, like they'd only recently been created, and they hadn't had time to be worn smooth from use.

I loved exploring potential secrets. What would this one reveal? I tried not to get my hopes up. Maybe I'd get it open and find a nest of spiders. Or nothing at all. It could be part of the original construction, or something added by a recent sentinel eager to create something new in the library.

After glancing around to make sure I was alone, though I supposed it shouldn't matter, I tucked my head back inside the opening. I pried at the edge of the door but other than breaking a nail, nothing happened.

I needed a tool to force it open.

I leaped to my feet and rushed to a desk, but despite searching the top and drawers, I didn't find anything I could use. Where was an ancient letter opener or nail file when a girl needed one?

A bang in the hallway outside the room made unease bolt up my spine. I rushed back to the opening and stuffed the books onto the shelf, trying to put them back in the same order I'd removed them, though I wasn't sure why. No one had said I couldn't explore in the library.

However, if something sneaky was going on here, I didn't want someone finding out I was on to their secret.

After making sure the area looked undisturbed, I scrambled across the room, grabbing a book from an upper shelf as I passed, and hopped onto a sofa. I stretched out, opened the book, and laid it pages down on my chest. I tipped my head back and ripped out a snore.

I'd get an A+ for drama. A C for my acting.

When I opened my eyes, Ressard stood beside the couch, frowning at me.

"You should rest in your room," he said, his lips slanting downward. "We discourage visitors from roaming the castle halls at night."

"Do you get many visitors here?" That was a new one for me. I hadn't seen anyone come near the castle.

"The sun has set. It would be best to remain inside your room for the night."

Yup. With a turned lock on my door.

"I fell asleep. I was worn out." By Venge, but I wasn't telling Ressard that. He didn't need to know what we were doing behind closed doors.

"Allow me to send a tray of food to your room," he

said pleasantly, though his intent gaze never left mine. "You will wait there for it."

In other words, leave the library, where they couldn't lock the door, and go to your room, where they could.

I sat and dropped the book on a nearby table. "Sure. I'll do that."

"Do you have any dietary preferences this evening?" he asked, his usually neutral mood shining through. "Is there anything you would like me to send to your room?"

I could think of a billion favorites I remembered from Earth, but I doubted the food synthesizer could make them.

"I'll leave that to you," I said, breezing past him.

He followed me all the way to my room. I was tempted to continue down the hall, fling open Venge's door, and call out his name, but I had a feeling I wouldn't find him nearby. He disappeared at night, and I had no idea where he went.

Sentinel duties, I assumed.

With a sigh, I opened my door and strode inside.

Ressard said nothing, just shut my door. A click told me he'd locked it.

A steaming tub waited for me near the windows. I grumbled, but a long soak would feel good.

After stripping, I settled into the tub, groaning in pleasure as the toasty hotness sunk into my bones. I was stiffer and sorer than I'd assumed, my body having received a solid workout in Venge's bed.

I wanted to do it again as soon as we could. Why had

he left while I was asleep? He should've awoken me, at least to say goodbye.

I climbed out of the tub and dried off, then strode to the closet, though I knew I didn't have much to wear. But I found a couple of dresses and decent replications of my jeans and tees hanging in the big open space. Thank you, Azareela. I doubted Ressard had played a role in my new wardrobe.

I tugged a dress over my head, skipping my undies, which no one had thought to replicate. Venge might prefer if I went without...

Assuming I saw Venge again. A silly thought on my part, but he kept disappearing. What if one time, he didn't reappear in the morning?

"Jeez, don't think like that," I whispered, pacing. He'd hired me for a job. He wouldn't take off in the middle of it. We were making progress with the culairs.

And we were growing closer ourselves.

Someone knocked on the door.

It was stupid to call *come in* when they held the control, penning me up in here.

The knob rattled. A warning? Naw, whoever it was must have been worried I still lounged in the tub.

The door slowly opened, and Azareela walked in with a tray perched on one hand. She smiled when she saw me wearing the dress. "You look beautiful. That is a wonderful color on you."

"Thank you." I struggled to hold in my resentment, a hard thing when she was being nice. But I didn't like being locked inside.

She shut the door and strode across the room to lower the tray onto a table. "You can sit here and look out the window as you eat. It is lovely tonight. No rain."

"A rare thing," I said.

"The weather here is atrocious."

"Yet you live here. Venge said he's a sentinel, guarding this part of the planet." Even as I said it, I realized how lame the statement sounded. I hadn't seen him doing any guard duties, though he could have a high-tech room where he did his job.

At night. That was it. He only worked at night, because . . . That's when aliens from other planets attacked. They couldn't see during the day.

And my imagination was dragging me down a tunnel with no end in sight.

"Vengestire said that, did he?" Azareela asked, her head tilting.

"Isn't it the truth?"

She bustled around the tray, lifting the cover, and straightening the tableware. "I've included wine." She tapped a glass and the small bottle. "I have heard Earthlings enjoy this beverage."

"Are you saying Venge doesn't do sentinel duty?"

"I would never say anything like that." With a nod at the tray, Azareela hurried past me. "Please call out if you need anything else. We'll collect the tray in the morning."

"Where is Venge?" I asked. "I'd like to speak with him if he's free."

I needed reassurance. We'd been together intimately, and he'd taken off before I woke up.

"I don't believe he can come to you at the moment. I'm sure you'll see him tomorrow." She opened the door and stepped out into the hall. "Goodnight."

She locked the door before I could reach it, but really, was I going to knock her over to "escape"? They shut me inside for a reason, though I had no idea what it was. After battling the creatures in the woods, I could see why they worried. Maybe something horrible stalked the castle corridors at night.

That's what Venge was doing: fighting them off, making things safe for the rest of us.

The idea was lame, but it was all I could grab onto.

I sat and ate, my body hungry after the day's exertions. When I'd finished, I took the knife included on my plate and slipped it under the mattress. I'd use it to pry open the hatch in the library tomorrow. The mysterious opening behind the bookcase needed to be explored.

After that, I paced the room. At this rate, I was going to wear a hole in the carpet.

That's when the cries of pain began again, echoing through the castle, ripping up my spine like claws.

My jaw clenched. I was tired of sitting—or pacing—around while wondering what in the world was going on.

One by one, I ran to the windows, finding them all locked. There had to be a way out of this room.

Did I dare break a pane? The roofline wasn't far above

my window. I could reach it. Once there, I could find a way to another room, one that didn't have a locked door.

I returned to the biggest window, but when I looked out, I spied someone far below, standing. A guard?

Maybe it was Verge.

But then the guy turned, and his face was revealed by moonlight.

Ressard.

He stared directly at my window. Watching.

23
VENGE

I felt like I walked on the edge between madness and salvation. I'd experienced the most joy in my life within Jenny's arms, but I'd had to leave her at sundown.

Walking away from my room, knowing she slumbered in my bed and would smile and reach for me if I woke her, was one of the hardest things I'd ever done.

But my skin was hardening, and I knew the nighttime beast would overtake my body before long. Each morning, this part of me retreated.

How long before the gargoyle remained, and I was lost forever?

It wasn't fair. No one should have to live like this. But each male of the third generation who'd lived here before me had withstood the onslaught until they finally succumbed. I could do nothing less than them.

I didn't wait for the gargoyle to finish claiming me but hurried down the back stairs to the lowest level. We'd installed a high-tech lock when we arrived, and the door opened to my touch. I didn't close it behind me, because Ressard would be along soon to ensure my chains had been secured.

I strode down the long hall lined with cells, aiming for the last, the one I'd staked out as mine when I arrived. Others had used these same rooms.

Died in these same rooms.

The idea of my death tasted bitter. I'd found a mate, someone to love. She'd given herself to me sweetly. I hated that I would lose this, that her memories would be chewed up and swallowed by the beast.

How long before I forgot who she was?

I'd been stupid to adopt culairs. I'd leave them just like I would Jenny. They bonded with one person, and it was clear Gular already favored me. Would he mourn me when I no longer arrived at the pasture?

I well knew why Fleese avoided me. Clever, he'd spied the gargoyle lurking inside me.

He shunned us both.

But at least he no longer tried to kill me. He glared and hissed, but kept his distance, watching with irritation while Gular and Jenny sat with me and adored me.

She *did* adore me; I could tell.

As I entered the last cell, I realized I'd done something truly terrible.

I'd made her love me.

It wasn't fair that this was happening to me, but it was even less fair to make her love me only to leave her so soon.

What if she carried my young already?

It was assumed the next victim of this tainted blood would come from my sister's great-great-grandson, but perhaps I'd set the next few generations in motion with Jenny.

Despite cursing myself for my actions, I couldn't stop seeking out her presence. I couldn't stop touching her. Loving her.

It was wrong to steal a bit of time with her, but I couldn't hold myself back. I might be doomed, but that didn't mean I couldn't fall in love.

"Let me help you," Ressard said from the open door to my cell. He approached me with great caution, watching my eyes for a hint I'd attack.

"I haven't succumbed," I said in a tired voice. "Not yet." I lifted my hands and secured the first cuff to my right wrist.

He attached the other and then bound my ankles, securing me to the wall for the night. By morning, I would hang here, spent from trying to rip free.

I hated this, hated what I was becoming, but it was a tidal wave, and I was a shell lying on the shore.

And after I'd returned to my rooms, Ressard would examine the spikes in the wall. I sometimes ripped them out. Eventually, he'd have to shut the door in case I broke completely free.

I couldn't be allowed to roam the castle halls.

Ressard scooted out the open archway and down the hall. The door at the end banged shut, locking me inside the cold dungeon.

I couldn't hold back any longer. My skin morphed,

stiffening along my arms in rippling waves. Turning me to flexible stone. Wings sprouted from my back, the spikes on the top of the segments stabbing against the wall. If I were free, would I be able to fly? Bound to the wall all the time, I had no way to test them.

As always, I abhorred this. Abhorred myself. If only I could stop it from happening. If only I had a way forward, a path that would take me past the beast lurking deep within my soul.

It was all I could do to hold onto me.

I tipped my head back and shrieked out my pain.

24
JENNY

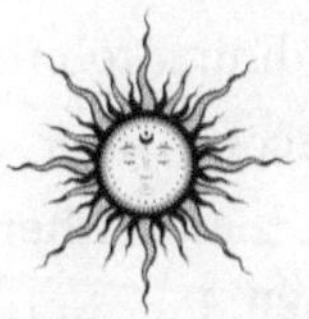

I couldn't sleep, not while someone was suffering.

Not while a *creature* was suffering. The cries didn't sound human. Or alien. They sounded like a beast being ripped apart from the inside out.

All my life, I'd struggled for freedom against the bonds my father chose to wrap around me. Even when he forced me to marry Thurston, I hadn't given up hope that I would get away. Through it all, the animals I worked with kept me from going out of my mind. Helping them and their owners gave me a purpose, a cause, and ultimately, the escape I sought for myself.

When the door unlocked, I rushed from the room, catching Ressard exiting from a door on the opposite side of the hallway from the main staircase.

I raced after him, determined to pin him down and make him answer some questions. But by the time I'd reached the door, he'd locked it.

Growling with frustration, I pivoted and slumped

against the panel. I glared down the hall, but there was no one I could direct my irritation toward.

I shoved off the surface and stomped along the carpet, my feet making dull thuds. I continued down the stairs to the first floor, determined to track down Azareela and make her give me some answers.

She wasn't in the dining room or the front parlors. I even raced to the second floor and dashed into the library, but she wasn't there, either. I was tempted to see if I could force the small door in the bookcase open, but I'd forgotten my hidden knife, and my driving need was to find someone to tell me what was going on.

I rushed from the library and slammed into someone in the hall.

Venge latched onto my arms, holding me steady.

"You," I said, short of breath from racing around.

He wore almost nothing, only a scrap of cloth wrapped around his waist to cover his groin. Sweat coated his body, and like days ago, red abrasions encircled his wrists and ankles.

"Who is tying you?" I snarled, guessing what the rings on his skin must mean.

His eyes widened. "Why would you think someone was doing something like that?"

"This." I pointed but didn't poke at the redness on his right wrist. I couldn't touch the raw area for fear of hurting him. "You didn't do this to yourself."

"Jenny. Don't ask me about this." Warning came through in his voice, but his tone remained gentle, not angry.

"Are you involved with whatever's going on at night here?"

He stilled, and his eyes slid away. If I didn't know this guy, I'd think he felt shame. "You should not ask."

"A creature is in incredible pain. Each night, it screams." My eyes stung with tears. "I want to help this animal. It needs me."

He took my hand and tugged me into the library, shutting the door behind us. Then he pulled me into his arms and held me.

"I wish I could tell you everything, but I cannot," he said, curling around me to lay his chin on the top of my head.

"A creature is suffering."

"You are correct."

"Why can't you tell me what it is and why it's suffering?" I tipped my head back, needing to watch his face, but it remained smooth, giving nothing away.

"Because I do not wish to lie."

I grabbed his hands and shook them, making him look at me. "Please."

He tugged one hand away and stroked my hair. "You are the loveliest person I have ever met. Do you know that I am falling in love with you?"

It was a distraction, but I couldn't help sliding into its embrace. "Venge." I tumbled into his arms and held him while he wrapped me up tight, as if he feared someone would wrench me away from him forever.

"I'm falling for you too," I mumbled against his skin. He drew a kaleidoscope of feelings from deep inside me.

So many emotions, I couldn't process them. But through it all, love shone through. "I'm sorry."

"Why?"

"For bugging you about this, for making demands."

"Be yourself, Jenny. That is all I need."

I wasn't sure I could let this go, but it was equally clear he didn't want to tell me anything. I could stop pressing him for answers or . . .

This wasn't only about satisfying my curiosity. If an animal was in pain and I could help it, I had to do so.

He leaned over and kissed me. Heat sparked between us like always. My body warmed, remembering how good it had been between us the day before. I wanted it like that again.

His hands roamed my spine slowly, as if he mapped my skin with his fingers. Memorized me. As his tongue teased across mine, a groan worked its way up from deep inside him, a precious gift released by his soul.

He swept me up and carried me to one of the big squishy chairs, where he sat, positioning me on his lap with my legs spread around his thighs.

"I have you where I want you, mate," he said with a grin. He fisted up my dress, his eyes widening when he saw I wore nothing beneath. "I truly do have you where I want you." He delved between my legs with his fingers, watching the passion growing on my face, a reflection of his need blooming inside me.

He rubbed my clit while sliding a knuckle inside me, the bent digit protecting me from the claw. Working me, he brought me to a writhing mess in no time. I was dripping, and he was panting.

I pushed aside the cloth covering his groin, revealing his already rock-hard cock. Thick veins stood out prominently along the sides, and like before, it felt almost like stone on the outside. It held so much stiffness, I could barely dent the skin with my fingertips.

I liked it this way. I needed to taste it.

When I eased off his lap, his finger slid from inside me, making a sucking sound. As much as I ached to feel him driving within me, I needed to take him into my mouth.

There was no way I could take him all, however. He was too long, too wide in girth. But I could give him joy, something I sensed he'd been denied most of his life.

I nudged his knees apart and moved between them.

He watched me with hooded eyes.

While his tail coiled around my leg, sweeping across my skin, making it tingle, I took him in my hands, sucking the end of his cock inside my mouth.

He growled and fisted my hair. "Mate."

I looked up at him, watching the myriad of expressions crossing his face. Excitement. Pleasure. Wonder. This was a little thing, but it was something I could do solely for him.

Well, me, too, since it was a big turn-on bringing him to the edge with my tongue and the suction of my mouth.

I moved my head up and down, mimicking my core cupping him deep within me, while his groans grew louder. He pumped his hips up to meet me, and there wasn't anything better than that.

His tail swished higher, a ticklish, firm thing. When it plunged inside me, I moaned. It was all I could do to remember what I was doing with my mouth. I wanted to lean forward and let his tail drive into me over and over, bring me to a screeching orgasm.

"Let me . . ." He tugged at my hair gently. "Mate. I need . . . I want . . ."

I released him, watching in satisfaction as his cock drove itself against his abs. "I think I know what you need." I climbed on top of him, his tail slipping from inside me, and centered his incredible length at my core.

He rubbed my clit, his other hand sneaking beneath my dress to fondle my breasts.

While he rolled my nipple and stroked my clit, I drove myself down on top of him, taking all of him with one thrust.

It felt wonderful. Sublime. As if we connected on a level we never had before.

As if we were one.

Heat flared in my heart, and it was echoed in my soul. I didn't know what it meant, but I knew I needed this.

Needed him and for so much more than sex.

My eyes rolled back as I started to move, lifting and allowing my body weight to shove me back onto his length.

He soon joined in on my rhythm, plunging up when I moved down.

The rhythm we took brought me closer and closer, but it didn't drive me all the way home. For that, I needed harder thrusts.

Whimpers rose in my throat.

Venge's tail took his finger's place on my clit, stroking and rubbing, while he grabbed onto my hips.

His body overcome with a fever, he took control, moving me up and down in almost a blur, giving me the driving force I'd sought all my life.

A scream worked its way up my throat, and when it released, the world would hear it. I didn't care. All I wanted was to feel his cock pushing deeply inside me.

"Mate," he growled. "I am close. You . . ." He shoved my dress to the side and curled forward to suck one of my nipples into his mouth, rolling it with his teeth while his tongue stroked the tip.

Shock waves blasted from my sensitive breasts to my core, pushing me all the way to the brink.

I fell apart in Venge's arms, my body shuddering with pleasure.

His body jerked beneath mine as he came along with me, shooting his hot seed deep within me.

"Should we be grateful no one in this castle but me seems to enjoy reading?" I mumbled against his skin.

He chuckled. "I enjoy reading."

"So many books. I haven't found any I could read, but there are some amazing pictures."

"This library has been added to for many years, each sentinel bringing his favorites with him."

"What books did you bring with you?"

"I didn't bring any."

A sense of hopelessness hung in the air around us, but I couldn't figure out why. What we'd just shared had been pristine. Full of power. I felt limp but like I could take on the universe and come up the victor.

I cupped his face. "Why not? Didn't you have any favorites?"

"So many, but . . ." His brow knit. "I guess I decided to read what was here, to explore the books those who were here before me treasured instead. As if by reading them, I could bring them back to life."

My heart pinched, though I didn't know why. "Venge."

His gaze met mine, and sadness flitted through his eyes. "What?"

"Everything feels tied together here."

"Maybe you hold the key?"

To what, though? If I could free whatever creature screamed at night, I would. "I want to help."

He rubbed my back. "Trust there isn't anything you can do. What is destined will come to pass, and like all those who lived here before me, I, too, will find my end."

"Not for a long time, though, right?" I needed his reassurance, him stating we had a long life together to look forward to.

Though in my heart, I already knew that wasn't true.

"I wish I could give you forever, mate," he said.

"You're saying we all die sometime."

"I don't speak of hypothetical things. I cannot share everything, but know in my soul, I will treasure you always. In my heart, you will be mine for this lifetime and beyond. That is the only forever I have to offer."

We'd just shared a precious moment, something to hold onto, but I could barely suppress my tears.

I felt like everything was collapsing around me, and there was no way to draw the edges back together.

25
VENGE

We spent the next few days working with the culairs.

"Would you look at that?" Jenny said with a grin. She sat beside me, leaning against my arm. "He loves you."

Gular lay sprawled on my lap, sleeping off the belly full of treats I'd given him.

Fleese crouched on the ground on the opposite side of Jenny, placid except for his intent expression trained on me.

Jenny lay back on the scraggly grass. Clouds drifted overhead, and it would be a perfect day if Fleese would soften fully, and I wasn't haunted by the cursed disease hanging over my head.

If only there was a way to end this, and I didn't mean by dying. I wanted to stay with Jenny. I hated that she'd wonder what happened to me.

I'd speak with Ressard later and ask him, when the

time came, to tell her I was mortally wounded. Perhaps by a creature in the forest. Or a fall.

He could tell her he was unable to recover my body.

A gruesome thing to do, but she would know I was gone and that I'd never return. She'd believe I didn't willingly leave her.

Jenny had collected long strands of vine dangling from one of the trees at the back side of the pen and was braiding them into one long strand, though I didn't know why. She seemed entertained by it, however, and who was I to deny her this joy?

We hadn't roamed the forest since the attack, not willing to risk endangering ourselves or the pups. Our walks had taken place in the vicinity of the castle.

"There's something else we could try with our recalcitrant pup," Jenny said, sitting up. She showed off the long braid before looping it around and around, forming a sequential circle. She tied it off at the top and set it aside.

"Giving Fleese back to his original owners?" I hated the idea of it, but how could I keep a pet who hated me?

"Not that," she said.

I stroked Gular's ears, and he sighed and butted my hand with his snout. His sleepy eyes met mine before his eyelids slid shut again. His snores echoed around us.

Fleese grunted and his scowl deepened, taking in Gular. I got the notion he was as irritated with his brother as he was with me. He must see this as Gular snuggling with the enemy.

A sense of desolation filled me. I didn't have much time left. Maybe it was a mistake to adopt pets I'd have to leave behind.

But I could stabilize, the beast may not progress. In the few books I'd found in the library—that I now kept in my room—I'd read of ancestors who'd gone into a remission period. One lasted twelve lunar cycles before his mind was completely taken over by the beast.

If only this could happen to me. Then Jenny and I would have more time together. I could make twelve lunar cycles feel like a lifetime. It might be enough.

I shook my head. That would never be enough when it came to Jenny. I'd always want more time with her.

Funny how much you regretted lost moments when your end was in sight. I couldn't go backward and find her long ago. All I could do was make the best of now.

"Fleese," Jenny said, tapping her thigh. "Come closer, little guy."

"Not so little," I said.

"He's a teensy baby." Her voice came out higher-pitched and cooing. She rubbed her fingers together. "Come on. Let me show you how amazing Venge is."

Fleese crept toward her, keeping his sharp gaze on me. He bared his fangs but didn't growl.

Good pup, I indicated with a narrowed gaze. If need be, two could bare their fangs and snarl.

Since Jenny had arrived and filled my world, the pups had grown, adding height and breadth. Would I live long enough to see them mature? What a sight that would be. They'd be bigger than me, even. Kreel and

Cora, the breeders of my pair, hooked the parents up to a cart and used them for transportation. Others rode culairs, and I couldn't imagine how wonderful that would be.

A bittersweet feeling filled me because I'd never know. Gular was tame enough I could ride him, but I'd be foolish to dream I'd be alive long enough to do so.

"Have you considered letting him sleep with you?" Jenny asked.

"Fleese?" I snorted, shaking my head. "I'd wake up with my arms burned off."

"Why not let him sleep with you tonight? Gular could too." She wiggled her eyebrows. "Me, if there's room with the culairs."

"I do not think this would work." I dragged my gaze from the questions lurking in her eyes.

There would be no sleeping for me for the rest of my days. Once the beast started to creep into my mind, I would already be locked away. When he filled me, I could barely think for myself.

There was no way these gentle culairs could remain near me when the gargoyle took over. If they saw what I became when my control slipped, they'd flee and never come near me again.

"Why not?" Jenny asked. "I've noticed you go somewhere the second the sun sets. Before, actually." A hint of hurt came through in her voice.

Despite my intention of never causing her pain, I did so by not telling her the truth. How could I, though? She wouldn't understand. She'd leave me, and I might be a horrible person for clinging, but I wasn't ready to let her go.

"I walk a lot at night." It was the best excuse I could come up with. "I can't sleep, so I pace. I don't want to disturb you."

"I thought you did sentinel duties."

"That involves walking." I hated being dishonest.

"The culairs would walk with you." Her hand slipped into mine. "So would I."

"You need your rest."

"I want to be with you."

"It is part of my . . . job." I hoped she didn't hear the hesitation in my voice.

The questions grew in her eyes. She'd demand answers soon, as she should, but I couldn't tell her the truth.

I would bear this alone.

Mostly alone. Azareela and Ressard were my conspirators on this journey.

Azareela provided companionship and the loving touch of a mother. She would not be able to kill me; she would leave that to Ressard. His family had chosen him for this role when he reached puberty. Those in his family saw it as an enormous honor.

I'd look him in the eye when he slid the blade through my heart. And if I could break through the beast's control, I'd voice my forgiveness. I didn't wish my friend to feel bad for completing the task he'd been given. Just as I and my ancestors succumbed to the gargoyle, Ressard's ancestors had granted us our final passage.

My heart twisted. I hated seeing her sad.

"You can walk with me someday, mate," I said, hedging. It was better to remain evasive than to outright lie.

"All right," she sighed, relenting, and leaned across me to stroke Gular's back.

Because I couldn't resist, I started nibbling on her neck.

She bit back a moan. "Venge." Humor came through the warning in her voice. "You're distracting me."

"Lay back in the grass, and I will give you pleasure." My cock jutted against my pants, eager.

"Someone could see us from a window."

"They are all busy."

She snorted and leaned against me. "You have no way of knowing that."

"I could demand they look away."

"You're not the demanding type."

I nudged her down onto the grass. "You think not, do you mate? Allow me to show you."

Her arms went around my neck, and she stroked my skin. I kissed her jaw, moving down toward her breasts. With a shift of my body, I shielded our actions from anyone who did happen to be looking out a window.

From the corner of my eye, I watched Fleese go still before creeping closer. Jenny was infinitely distracting. I ached to glide my fingers beneath her skirt and see if I could make her moan some more, but Fleese . . .

I stretched out my hand toward him, and he sniffed

it. He lifted his head, and for a moment, his gaze seemed to soften. We were making progress. I might yet tame this tiny beast before . . .

No, I was not going to think of that today. I'd dwell on it soon enough when I was closer to the complete change. Today was for me and Jenny.

And Gular and Fleese.

Jenny's fingers trailed down my chest and beneath my shirt, where she glided the soft tips across my nipples.

It was more a sensing than seeing, but I felt parts of me shifting to the stone being I would soon become. The *gargoyle*.

Fleese froze. Growling, he backed away. I realized this was why he avoided me, why he hated me. He saw who I struggled not to become.

How could I tell him I'd never hurt him when once the gargoyle took full charge, this body would go on a rampage?

"So close," Jenny said, watching Fleese. "Tomorrow, he'll come near again and this time, he'll lick your fingers."

He'd never lick my fingers. He'd never trust me.

I tucked my arm behind my back, heat climbing from my chest to my face. "You are right. Soon, he will like me."

Despite my attempt to sound hopeful, the dead feeling growing inside me came through in my voice.

No matter how hard I tried to hold it back, the change was happening.

Would Jenny scream if she saw my skin morphing to stone? I couldn't bear to frighten her.

This was why all my ancestors had been locked away until the end.

And why they'd been put out of their misery not long after that.

26

JENNY

Venge disappeared before dinner. But then, the sun had set.

He had to *walk*. Do sentinel things.

I wanted to believe his words, to think of him striding through the woods—safely—while walking off whatever haunted him through the night.

But the start of disbelief crept through my heart.

There was another reason, one he didn't want to share. It hurt, though I sensed he didn't withhold information because he didn't trust me.

Strangely enough, I got the idea he didn't share because he was ashamed of what he would have to tell me.

After putting the rope I'd made from vines inside my room, I went down to the dining room. I'd probably never need the rope, but having it made me feel like I had a way out.

Thoughts about what might be going on with Venge

spiraled through me as I sat at the table, eating alone. Azareela watched, but despite me practically begging her to join me, she refused, mumbling something about needing to attend to things in other parts of the house. She soon left the room and didn't return.

Pushing aside my unfinished plate, I left the dining room. I didn't want to be locked inside my room yet, so when I heard footsteps in the hall coming my way, I scooted from the dining room and into one of the parlors. From there, I'd discovered, I could traverse the right side of the castle without taking the hall, using doors connecting one room to another.

In the third room, I came across the list of names covered with a drape again.

I traced my finger along the most recently etched name, Vengestire Rarkeleone Abesteen, then studied each of the others that appeared above his, though I doubted I'd learn anything new from the list.

Only one name stood out among the rest, because someone had added a tiny etched sword beside it.

Tellesandrus Raginmund Abesteen. Was he related to Venge? Why put a mark next to his name but no others?

Another mystery to add to the rest.

Were these the names of the sentinels who'd served life sentences here in the castle? It wouldn't be unusual to honor them by creating a plaque like this.

I wanted to believe this was a true job, one he'd agreed to complete, though I couldn't imagine how lonely it must be for those sent here.

No, there was something else going on; something I was missing.

Which reminded me of the hidden compartment in the library. With Azareela distracted and Ressard nowhere in sight, it was the perfect time to pry open the tiny hatch.

I didn't dare return to my room for the knife, worried I'd be seen entering and they'd scurry up behind me and lock me inside.

I studied the room with the plaque, noting a fancy desk standing in the corner. When I searched it, I found something vaguely resembling a ruler. It had a fine edge that almost cut my finger when I pressed down on it hard. Was it thin yet strong enough to pry open the hatch?

There was only one way to find out.

Remembering the locked stairwell on my floor, I continued through the rooms all the way to the end of the building, hoping to find and use the stairs to climb to the second floor.

At the last room, I was forced to exit out into the hall. Left would take me back to the foyer. I continued right, to the door at the end.

Not locked. Yay.

Inside, I found the stairwell and continued up to the second floor. I peeked out the door, and when I found the hall clear, I hurried down it, then crossed a long, open balcony area to the other side, where the library was located.

The library was dark, but the moon had risen,

shining light through cracks between the drapes. Since I didn't dare turn on a light and risk being discovered, I scurried along that wall full of glass, pulling aside all the curtains.

With the added light, I could see quite well. I dropped to my knees beside the stack and started tugging out books, layering them beside me.

When I'd revealed the section I sought, I edged my upper body inside the opening, the "ruler" tight in my hand. I stuffed it into the gap between the small hatch and the back of the bookcase, grateful it fit in the opening.

After all it took to get to this moment, I expected to find this yet another challenge. But with a little wiggling, the hatch slid to the side, revealing a compartment no larger or deeper than the length of my forearm.

"Stuff your hand into the dark and see what happens," I whispered. A hysterical giggle slipped from my mouth before I slapped my hand over it. Jeez. I was going to scare myself. Did I think an alien spider could get inside a tiny space that didn't appear to have been opened for years?

A growl slipped from my throat.

I leaned down land peered into the opening, waiting for my eyes to adjust to the darkness.

Something flat lay on the bottom. I removed a book and dropped it with the others, then looked inside again, finding nothing else in the tiny area.

I huffed and closed the hatch, stacking the books

back on the shelf—all except the one I'd found. That, I'd take to my room to examine.

With the book tucked between my arm and chest, I stood.

That was when the cries began once more, echoing through the castle passages. I didn't like thinking there was a connection between Venge disappearing and an animal bellowing in pain, but what else could I suspect?

However, I wasn't locked inside my room. There was no harm in checking this out.

I took the back stairs to the floor with my rooms, my thighs burning. Truly, if I lived here, I'd install some kind of lift. What did people do when they got old? They couldn't expect an eighty-year-old to do a workout like this on a regular basis. What if they twisted their ankle? Someone would have to carry them up and down the stairs.

Carrying a book up all these flights was enough for me.

I didn't find anyone waiting in the hall, and I had to wonder where Ressard and Azareela had disappeared to. I wasn't going to seek them out, however. They'd find me sooner than I'd like.

Because the door at the top of the stairs was locked, I grabbed an urn sitting on a low table nearby and placed it in the opening, keeping the door from fully closing. Then I scurried to my room.

I tucked the book under my mattress and crept back down the hall to the stairs, returning the urn to the table to keep others from becoming suspicious.

It was only a hunch on my part, but I suspected the stairs might lead me to where the animal cried out in pain. There was no access to lower levels from the staircase in the foyer.

The cries grew louder as I descended, and I froze every other step, wondering if this was the stupidest thing I'd done in my life. Whatever lurked below could hurt me. I should rush back up the stairs and this time, hide in my room until they locked me up for the night.

Creatures roam the castle at night–Azareela had told me that.

What if they locked my door so that whatever bellowed couldn't reach me?

My skin prickled with fear, but I kept descending. The heavy thrum of my heart echoed in my ears, almost overwhelming the cries that grew louder as I made my way down into the bowels of the castle.

Back on Earth, castles often had dungeons. Would I find one here?

My mouth had gone dry, and terror prickled through me.

A clinking sound rang out from ahead, followed by more cries.

I froze, truly wondering if I had the strength to keep going. But I had to know what was happening. If an animal needed help, I wanted to give it. I needed to make a difference.

When I reached the bottom of the stairs that bottomed out on a wet, slick stone floor, I found an open archway with a door cracked open. Dark gloom greeted me. Would it hurt anyone to install some lights?

Still, my eyes adjusted to the muted light coming in from slices of windows high on the right walls of the passage. I was able to make out a long hallway with barred rooms on either side.

I nudged the door fully open, grateful it didn't creak to reveal my presence. Silence reigned, and I began to believe I'd headed in the wrong direction.

Until a clink and a groan rang out ahead.

I crept forward, keeping my footsteps light, peering into each barred room—no cell—on either side, finding all of them empty. Rusty chains hung from the walls, though. Had people been incarcerated here in the past?

One longer room spanned the end of the hall, and I could tell there was no way out other than by the way I'd entered.

Pausing, I listened, but I didn't hear anything but low breathing ahead.

Ugh. I should run back upstairs.

I tiptoed forward toward the last cell in the hall, unsure what I'd find, but determined to see this through.

As I moved closer, I swore the breathing stilled, as if whatever was inside the cell heard me and didn't wish to make a sound.

There was nothing that would induce me to call out "hello." I'd seen enough horror vids to know I needed to keep quiet.

Beasts hunted in the dark.

With extraordinarily little light from the moon, it

was almost impossible to see, which could be the whole point of this. Maybe whatever lurked here didn't wish to be seen.

A silly thought on my part, but it stuck.

Because I didn't like remaining out in the open where anything could find me, I moved over to the right wall, hugging the bars as I continued forward. Soon, I'd know what everyone was determined to keep hidden. Was whatever waited in the cell the reason Venge was forced to remain at the castle?

In addition to being a sentinel, he could be a caretaker, though I had no idea what he might be taking care of.

When I was within a foot or so of the cell wall, I stopped, squinting to see inside the space.

An animal—no, a creature—was chained to the back of the room. A stone being who didn't seem to know I was here.

It tipped its head back and roared with pain.

My skin quivered with goosebumps, and my heart beat furiously against my ribs. Every instinct inside me told me to run and never return to this dungeon.

I tried to make out the creature's features, realizing I'd seen something similar in a book about ancient buildings in France.

A gargoyle? An alien gargoyle, that was. The stone creature had wings, though they didn't extend because they were pressed between his body and the wall. Horns jutted from the beast's head. Long fangs glistened in the low light.

Its body appeared to be made of flexible stone.

It raged, yanking on the chains while gnashing its fangs.

I jumped when it shrieked, and its cry cut off. It lifted its head, nostrils flaring while its glowing eyes sought me where I hid in the shadows.

Pivoting on my heel, I bolted. I rushed down the hall and took the stairs faster than I had in my life.

I didn't stop running until I'd shut the door to my rooms behind me.

While the cries of the gargoyle echoed around me, I huddled on my bed, shivering beneath the blankets.

27

VENGE

"You almost lost control last night," Ressard said with sorrow. He unlocked the manacle binding my right wrist to the wall, then my left.

"I *did* stay in control." I hoped I did, that is. I couldn't remember. This was new. And frightening. "I am still bound. I am myself again. The beast did not fully take over."

"It is true. You did not break free," he said.

Panic filled me at the thought that soon, Ressard would arrive in the morning to find the beast waiting. Then he'd take the knife used on all my ancestors and end this.

End *me* forever.

I wasn't ready, although who could prepare for something like this?

"You won't be safe much longer," Ressard said. His eyes wouldn't meet mine, but the slump of his shoulders told me how sad he was about this. "I'm sorry."

"I will hold it back," I said as he undid my ankles. "I will not turn."

I stepped forward, pausing to rub my abraded flesh and flex my muscles. As much as I was grateful I couldn't hurt anyone when I changed, I hated being bound. It dehumanized me, a term that shouldn't apply to any species that wasn't human, but still did.

"You know the time will come when morning arrives, but you remain locked within the beast," he said softly from behind me. "It will not be long now."

I turned to face him, finding only dismay in his eyes. "I need more time." So much more.

"I understand, but it isn't meant to be. You know this. The beast knows this. Don't wait until it has been too long."

He meant until I raged through the dungeon, slamming against walls and trying to claw my way out. "I won't."

"This Earth female you have brought here. She is a complication," he said. "After what happened . . ."

"To Tellesandrus."

"Yes."

Only one of my ancestors hadn't been killed here inside the castle when he was completely consumed by the gargoyle. It was many generations in the past, when a small group of people lived in a nearby village. After what happened, they all fled, and if they were wise, they'd traveled to the other side of the planet or boarded spaceships and left altogether.

Tellesandrus fell in love with a female and she with

him. They fled before he'd fully changed, and when he did, he murdered her and then himself.

None of us since wanted to risk something like that happening again.

When I hired Jenny, I didn't think I'd fall in love with her.

"You need to send her away," Ressard said.

"I could go into remission."

"That is rare."

"Not impossible." With desolation filling me, I stomped back and forth in front of him. "The curse could end on its own."

"That has never happened."

But it could. Then I'd have more time with my mate. I wouldn't need to die soon.

I could hold the beast off forever if it meant I could spend even one more day with Jenny.

But what if I couldn't contain this? What if I broke free from the wall and escaped the dungeon?

I could hurt the culair pups, Ressard, or my aunt.

It would kill me if I even scratched Jenny.

She'd see me in that form. She'd know what I was. That would be worse than dying.

Ressard grunted. "If you want, I could take you some-place else where I could . . ."

Kill me.

I swallowed, not liking this idea any more than sending Jenny away.

"She could then remain here and care for the culair pups until we found them a new home," he continued.

Ressard could be persuasive.

"When?" I asked.

His gaze narrowed on me as if assessing me, but I'd already looked. None of my limbs remained molded into stone. "A few more days?"

So soon. It wasn't enough, but then, there would never be enough to satisfy my need to be with my mate.

"All right," I said, my chest as tight as if a boulder sat on it. "At least I have a bit more time." I would fill each day with happiness. I would claim her body and give her so much pleasure, she'd never forget me.

"I hope you have more time, my friend," Ressard said, patting my shoulder. "I believe we can give you this. Enjoy this time with her. I can tell you love her."

"I do," I said, not feeling shame at the tears filling my eyes. "I will until my final day."

28

JENNY

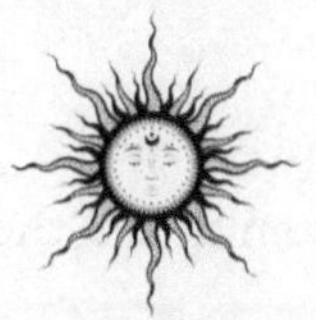

I tossed and turned all night, only drifting to sleep sometime before dawn. In my dreams, the creature I'd seen in the basement chased me, its eyes glowing with fury, its claws extended.

Sometimes, people were better off not knowing secrets. In trying to solve this mystery, I'd unveiled something I had no idea how to handle.

So much for me being a beast tamer. The first true beast I come across, I run away from. But what should I have done? Striding over to the creature would have been stupid. It could break its chains. Grab me.

Kill me.

Yet I couldn't stop thinking about returning to the basement the next chance I got. The creature was quiet during the day; perhaps it slept. If I tiptoed down there again during that time, I could look into the situation. I might be able to make a difference.

I woke early the next morning and tugged the book out from underneath the mattress.

Laying it on my lap, I realized there may be nothing exciting within this tome. It could contain recipes or garden plots. I'd be silly to think it held clues about the beast I'd seen downstairs or what was happening inside the castle.

I flipped it open and grinned.

Someone had written this in the universal language. I could read it.

However, the book had been damaged by water, though I had no idea how. I doubted it rained in the back of the bookcase.

"A journal," I whispered, leaning over to see. Even with daylight filtering in through the window, the writing was a challenge to read.

Today was my first . . . here.

"Nothing exciting about that." I continued to read, though many words had blurred beyond legibility.

From pouring over each page initially but then skimming to see if there was anything good, I learned the following.

Tellesandrus Raginmund Abesteen—the guy with the tiny sword beside his name on the plaque downstairs —was the author of the journal.

He'd come here when he was twenty-eight-years or cycles or whatever they called it old.

He identified himself as a sentinel sent to guard the castle, though he put sentinel in quotes.

Did he hate the job for dragging him away from his

other life? Or was there another reason to highlight his position?

I continued to skim.

He'd hated it here. It rained a lot. He was lonely. The staff did their best to keep him comfortable, but he felt as if his fate was "inevitable."

What fate was that? It appeared all the sentinels felt doomed. They might feel that way since they were forced to do a job with no way out except death.

I couldn't imagine what they'd been sent to guard. This scraggly rock of a planet couldn't be worth much.

After this, Tellesandrus went a long stretch without updating the journal. I could tell by the numbers on the top of the page.

When he started writing again, he was excited. He'd visited the village and met a female. She called to him like no other, and he had hope she felt the same.

Two more lunar cycles passed before he wrote again.

He and the female were meeting secretly. He was in love. She'd triggered his true mate bond. How did that differ from a regular mating?

They were planning to run away . . .

Why run? As far as I could tell, there were no rules in the "sentinel" handbook that forbid the sentinel from being with someone. Venge was with me. Sure, we hadn't talked about marriage or anything like that, but I got the idea that he saw a future for us.

This wasn't just a quick fling on his part.

Definitely not on mine. I wanted everything. A

marriage or mating, whatever he wanted to call it. A family.

A long life together.

Still, he must've felt he couldn't have that with her while serving as the sentinel. Perhaps her family forbid them from being together. That could explain why they felt they had to run.

The dates advanced, suggesting a few weeks passed before he wrote again. And this was his final. All the pages after it were blank.

I have found a way, and it lies with her. My staff don't . . . The last bit of the paragraph was smeared and unreadable.

There were only two more lines in the journal.

I will hide this book, hoping . . . find it. There is hope. Only with her in my life can I . . . it.

Trust in your true mate. It is the cure. You . . . need . . . die.

I flipped the page again, hoping I was mistaken, that I'd missed something.

"More," I growled. "I need more. This doesn't make sense. What did he trust in? And what does the cryptic comment about death mean?"

I tossed the book onto the covers and flopped back on the pillows, staring up at the canopy drapes.

If anything, the journal only created more questions.

Why had Tellesandrus and his love needed to run? What was a true mate?

And what did he mean when he spoke of dying?

I'd read the journal again tonight, hoping to find

something I'd missed, but for now, it appeared this was a lost cause. All that effort to sneak back to the library, and I'd learned nothing substantial. I'd search the hole behind the bookcase another time in case there was something I'd missed. Like, maybe another journal, one continuing where this one left off.

Tellesandrus assumed hiding the journal would do something. Did he expect other sentinels to find it? If so, why not leave it out on a desk?

It made no sense.

I got out of bed and dressed. I'd bathe after dinner. For now, I wanted to find Venge.

When I reached the dining room, he stood on the other side of the table, waiting.

"You should've come upstairs," I said with a wink, lowering my voice, though there was no one else in the room. "I didn't sleep in. You could've joined me."

"I had things to take care of this morning." He came around the table and lifted me up for a long kiss, but his face remained solemn after, his eyes shadowed.

"What's wrong?" I asked.

"Nothing I want to bother you with."

"Sentinel duties?"

He hesitated. "Yes, that."

I sat at the table and tugged over a tureen full of something that vaguely resembled scrambled eggs but could actually be fruit. Nothing was the same here when compared to Earth, but everything tasted good, and it filled me up.

"What do you guard?" I asked, scooping up some of

the "eggs." I watched what I was doing, but I also watched him.

"What do you mean?"

"Does the planet hold resources others would kill to steal? I don't see crops here that won't grow elsewhere unless the trees are important. I'm just curious about why this planet needs a lifetime guard."

"You guessed right," he said, taking a slice of bread and dropping it on his plate. He focused on adding something jam-like to the slice, though the "jam" could taste like meat for all I knew. "The sentinel guards a particular . . . species that cannot survive anywhere else."

"Like the beast in the basement."

His hand stilled, and his piercing gaze met mine. "What are you talking about?"

"I, um . . ." Heat filled me, and I squirmed in my chair. Maybe I shouldn't mention sneaking around last night. But this was Venge. I was in love with him. I didn't want secrets between us. "I found a second staircase last night after dinner. I followed it down."

"You shouldn't explore inside the castle."

"Or outside, for that matter, considering what stalks the woods."

"That either."

"I've heard cries of pain every night. I was curious." I slumped, feeling like I'd made a huge mistake. Not for seeking out the cries, but for telling Venge.

"I ask you not to look into this further," he said, lifting the slice of bread. He took a big bite and chewed, speaking around it. "The castle holds dangers I cannot explain. If you were hurt . . ." He shook his head, and pain cratered his face. "I would do anything to keep that from happening. Please."

I swallowed, coughing because my throat was so dry. A drink of water didn't help.

"I'm sorry," I said. "I want to know what's going on. What is that creature chained in the basement?"

"Something you don't want to meet. Ever." He placed his half-eaten bread on his plate. "Please don't pursue this."

"All right. I'll let it go."

Bringing up the book didn't feel wise at the moment. My heart pinched tight, and it hurt to breathe.

I just wanted things right between us again.

I reached across the table, grateful when his hand met mine halfway. We linked our fingers, and I marveled again at how much bigger he was than me. With one swipe of his arm, he could kill me.

But I knew in my bones he would die rather than do something like that.

"Take a walk with me?" he asked after we'd finished.

I took his hand. "Sure. Inside or out?" A silly question. He wouldn't want to stroll around inside the house.

"Out."

I'd snooped enough, and I wouldn't do so again. It wasn't solely about disappointing him. I'd decided that maybe things would go better for me if I behaved. For a while at least.

We strode down the halls to the left side of the building and exited beneath the approximate location of the library.

Should I mention the book?

Probably, but he kept grinning my way slyly, and I suspected he had something fun planned. Mentioning his ancestor's cryptic words could ruin this moment.

We walked into the woods, though this section had been cut and only a few spindly trees grew among the high bushes. A path wove among them, leading away from the castle.

We emerged out into a big open field with a long row of tall hedges.

"A maze?" I said in awe, coming to a halt.

"Would you like to walk through it with me?" he asked, his eyes sparkling with excitement.

"What waits in the middle?"

"You'll have to hold on tight," he lifted our linked hands, "and wait to see. If you behave, there will be a treat for you at the end."

My body simmered. I knew what treat I'd like to share with Venge.

"Lead away. I'll behave." I grinned. "Promise."

"Not too much, I hope," he said, guiding me into the flower-covered, arched opening. He took a right and led me down a long passage with vines growing in profusion around us, some even dangling off the hedges.

When he noticed I had to jog to keep up with him, he slowed his pace.

"You're quiet today," I said. "Are you feeling all right?"

"I am well. As well as I can be." He led me around a corner and halfway down another stretch, taking a right through an opening halfway to the end. We walked through a series of passages and turns, until it was clear I'd never find my way out alone. I wasn't scared. Venge was with me, and he'd keep me safe.

After twenty minutes or so, we left the mesh of maze and stepped out into an open area in the middle. A pile of furs lay on the ground near a bottle of this planet's version of wine, plus two glasses.

"Oh, please tell me you plan to seduce me," I said with a laugh.

He tugged me around to face him and stroked my shoulders. "Perhaps I would like you to seduce me."

I leapt into his open arms. "Any time."

He lifted me up and kissed me, and it wasn't long before I was pressing against him and moaning. Would it always be like this between us? I hoped so.

He continued kissing me while striding over to the furs. But before he lowered me onto them, he placed me on the ground and carefully sliced off my clothing with his claws.

"Hey," I said, my breathing feverish and my heart slamming in my chest. I was wet for him already and couldn't wait for him to claim me. "I'll need that dress when I walk back to the castle. No need to put on a show."

He waved to a pile of clothing I'd missed resting on the ground near the hedge wall. "I thought of everything."

"Then do whatever you want with me," I said with a smile, backing onto the furs. Oh, how lush they felt beneath my feet, silky and smoother than the softest down. I couldn't wait to lie back on them while Venge rose above me.

He scooped me up and kissed me again, bringing me to a moaning wreck. My legs wrapped around him, and I ground myself against his chest.

"Impatient little thing, aren't you?" he said, laying me on the furs and rising over me. "Have you behaved, mate?"

"I have," I said, enjoying this game.

"Then you shall have your reward."

He scooted lower and lifted my legs up, hitching them on his shoulders. While his soft tail stroked my thighs, gliding up my belly to my breasts, Venge licked me, sucking at my juices. He stroked my clit with the tip of his finger while his tail spiraled around to delve deeply within me.

My eyes rolled back in my head, and I whimpered, needing this but so much more. I was never going to get enough of this guy; I'd accepted this as a fact.

He was the stars and the moons to me. I'd give almost anything to make him happy, to see him at peace.

I clung to his hair, tugging yet holding his mouth against my body.

He pulled back with a chuckle that was so full of heat, it transfused from him to my soul. "You want me."

I nodded, unable to say a word. It was so much more than want. What we created together arced across my soul and gave me a feeling of completeness I'd never experienced in my life.

He rose above me and placed his cock at my opening. "You need this."

I nodded faster.

"I will give you everything you need, mate." He plunged inside me, so fast and hard I gasped.

He paused and looked down at me. "Pain?"

"Never. Don't stop." My gaze blurred. All I could focus on was the feel of him filling me, the throb of his cock deep within me.

He started moving, soon going faster at my urgings. We spiraled, soaring so high, I didn't think I'd ever return to the ground. It would always be like this between us. I knew this in my soul.

We came together, our cries echoing in the small open area.

His cock expanded to lock him within me. He rolled, taking me with him to put him on the bottom with me lying on top.

I kissed his chest.

"You make life worth living, mate," he said in a deep voice full of emotion. "I cannot go on without you."

"Same." I kissed his chest again. He was so much

taller than me, I couldn't reach his lips until his cock unlocked, but his chest was nice. He had defined muscles I savored licking.

Vulnerability flashed through me, though I had no idea why. Our future might not be set in stone, but it existed. We just had to hold on to each other and stay on the ride.

A look I couldn't define crossed his face. "Mate." Endless sorrow came through in his tone.

I didn't like it, and I didn't want to ask, but I couldn't help it. Something else was going on, and I had to know.

"What's wrong?" I asked.

"I don't know how else to say this."

The devastation in his eyes made my heart come to a shuddering stop. I sucked in a breath, wheezing, because I suspected what he was going to say.

He'd never promised me forever.

No! I couldn't take it. I couldn't—

He cupped my face, his fingers carefully tracing along my cheeks, and stared into my eyes. "I will have to leave you soon."

29
VENGE

"What do you mean?" she asked with a croak. Tears shimmered in her eyes, and I'd put them there.

I'd driven us to this point, and there was no way out.

Was it wrong to pursue her when I knew the end would have to come? The self-disgust roaring through me told me yes. I'd been greedy, grasping for something I could never have.

"My position here will end soon." I hated the lies, hated that I couldn't be truthful with her. But I'd seen the fear in her eyes this morning when she talked about the monster she'd encountered in the dungeon.

Before I sought her for this walk, I'd ensured the locks were secure and that she could never return to that level of the castle.

Not that it truly mattered. I would take Ressard up on his offer of moving me to a secure location. There, the beast would take full control of my mind and body.

There, I would die.

"I'll go with you," she said. "Wherever you go."

"I told you this position was for life."

"I don't get it." Tears streaked down her face and landed on my chest. "You're still young. You could do this job for a long time. I'll stay with you. Please."

My body unlocked from hers, and I sat, turning her to face me so I could hold her while she sobbed.

"I'm sorry." There wasn't anything else I could say. "I thought I had longer, that *we'd* have longer."

She leaned back in my arms. "I don't understand. Explain. There has to be a way." Her face froze. "Unless you're saying you don't want me any longer."

"Mate," I said, punctuating the endearment with a kiss. "I will want you forever. You are everything to me. So special and precious. I wish I had a lifetime with you."

"Tell me what's going on." Her voice came out shallow, soft, hesitant. "I want to understand."

How much could I tell her? I wanted to share everything, but from the moment I arrived on this planet, I'd been instructed by Ressard to keep it between him, my aunt, and me. He didn't indicate why; he just said that was how it had always been done. That only one person broke that rule and look what happened to him.

He and the female had fallen in love, and he'd killed her and himself.

I'd ruined our moment—what could be our final moment. But keeping my departure from her was wrong.

We dressed, saying nothing. It wasn't until we'd left

the maze and were walking along the trail in the woods that she spoke.

"When? How much time do we have?" She turned a tear-streaked face to me. "I accept that you can't tell me why this is happening. I don't understand, but I accept it. I don't want conflict between us when we have so little time left. I want to spend every moment with you until you—" Her voice choked off, and she dragged her gaze from mine to the path in front of us. "Until you have to leave."

"One day. Two, perhaps."

Her breath caught, and she stopped, her eyes pinching shut. "That's not enough time." She shook her head, holding up her hand before I could speak. "I'm sorry. Back in the middle of the maze, I told myself I wouldn't make demands, that I would do my best to accept what you could offer, but I thought there would be more."

"I give you everything I am, mate. All of me. All I have to offer. But in this, I have no choice. I'm rushing toward a cliff, and there's no stopping me from plunging over the edge."

"I would thrust myself between you and that cliff if it would save you."

I gathered her close, holding her. My body was all I had left to offer, and that would never be enough. How could it be when we had so little time?

"Why?" she mumbled against my skin. Her knees crumpled, and I held her, keeping her from falling. "Why, Venge?"

I didn't have an answer.

30
JENNY

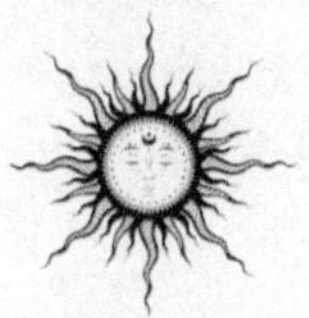

We retreated to his room and made love again, our touch feverish, desperate.

The sun was drifting lower, approaching the horizon.

He'd leave me soon, and though I tried to make each second matter, they slipped away like dandelion fluff blowing in the wind.

I lay in his arms. I clung to him. But I wasn't strong enough to keep him here with me. No one possessed that strength.

I couldn't understand any of this. Why did he have to die, and why so soon? It didn't make sense but pestering him wasted the slice of time we still had together.

"Will you take the culairs when you leave here?" he asked, his voice muffled in my hair.

Accepting something that meant he was never coming back.

"To Earth?" I asked, struggling to sound normal. I wanted to sob. If I didn't hold it together, I'd beg.

"If Earthlings will accept them."

"I don't want to go back there. My father and my ex will be waiting. I'd thought I'd have time to figure out where I wanted to go after this job was finished. Can I stay here?" At least here, Venge's memory would be with me. I'd walk the halls like old people did when the love of their life had died—hearing the departed one's voice calling through the passages.

"You can't," he said. "You'll have to leave not long after me. You can go wherever you want. I'll make that possible."

"I have money. That's not the issue." We hadn't discussed my past much. I'd preferred to put it behind me, and it never felt significant enough to bring up. I'd wanted to live in this moment with Venge.

"There are many colonies where you would be safe. The culairs too."

"I'll take them with me. I know you'll worry about them if I don't."

His hands smoothed along my spine, his fingertips teasing. "I thank you."

My eyelids were heavy from crying, but I'd made myself stop. The last thing I wanted was to spend this final night together sobbing.

"I'm going to stay with you tonight," I said. "We're not leaving this room, not even to eat. Azareela can send trays up for us."

"I can't remain with you tonight, mate."

Again, his gaze flicked away from mine.

"Why?" I kept my voice neutral; I wouldn't whine.

But truly. If he was going to die tomorrow, why couldn't we have tonight? "I don't get it. This job can't mean this much. No one would expect you to spend the final night of your life patrolling . . . whatever you patrol." I bit back the other things I wanted to say.

I need you.

I love you.

I can't bear to let you go.

Fuck it.

"Don't leave me. Please," I said. I'd regret it for the rest of my life if I didn't beg. "I love you. I want to be with you always. I'll do whatever I have to do to be with you longer."

He rolled me over, rising above me. "I will remain with you for as long as I can. I can't promise anything more."

It made no sense. I could rail about it, or I could take what he offered and hold onto it forever.

But man, did it taste bitter. It wasn't fair. He was healthy. We were young. We should have long lives together. It was wrong that fate seemed determined to deny this to us.

"Let's run away," I said, remembering Tellesandrus's journal. "You might not be the first to take off with someone you love."

He frowned. "What do you know about that?"

"Tellesandrus? That he and a female he loved ran away. He didn't stay here to face this useless death the fates offered."

"He and his lover died."

My breath stilled. "What do you mean?" I struggled to remember the wording on the last page of the journal, but I couldn't bring it to mind. My head ached from crying and stress, and there was no reason to memorize something that couldn't help me and Venge.

"He . . ." His eyes pinched shut, and when he opened them, they shimmered with tears. "He killed her before he was claimed himself."

"Claimed . . ."

"Killed."

I struggled to ignore the first part of this, that he'd murdered the female he'd obviously loved. I didn't know him, but from his journal, I was convinced he would never do something like that to her. "Killed you said. He didn't die?" Like Venge said he would. "Who's going to murder you?"

He rose from the bed and crossed to look out the window. While I could appreciate the defined muscles he displayed when he was naked, I would not be distracted from this.

"Who is going to murder you, Venge?" I asked, sliding off the bed. "Tell me."

"I cannot."

"Tell me! If I can understand, I can . . ." I shook my head. "I don't know what. Be there with you?" As if I could stand by and watch him die? No, not die, be murdered. "You have to tell me. I love you, and I need to know."

He partly turned toward me, and his swallow went on forever. "I have a disease."

"What kind of disease?"

"A fatal one. It will torture me until…"

"Until someone kills you. Who's going to do it? Ressard, Azareela, or someone I haven't met?"

"It doesn't matter."

"It does to me!" I tugged on his arm, but he wouldn't turn to face me. "There must be a cure."

"There never has been. Every few generations in my family, the gene skips something needed. I can't explain that part other than with that because I don't understand it myself. We die, and it's pure torture. To keep from doing what Tellesandrus did with the female he loved, we come here. We remain here until the disease starts to take us."

"And then someone kills you."

"It's that or torture."

I couldn't bear for him to be tortured but dying couldn't be the answer.

"You're sure Tellesandrus killed his lover?"

"It's a known fact."

"Did they find the bodies?"

He said nothing, just stared out the window. The sun had dropped beneath the trees, slaking light through the upper branches. Soon, it would slip from view.

Venge would leave me, and then he would die.

"Without bodies, I'm not sure I believe it happened," I said.

"We don't need bodies to know how Tellesandrus's story turned out," he said softly. He finally turned and held my hands, squeezing them. "I will leave before I risk your life."

"Is the disease contagious?"

"It's a genetic thing, passed down to the males of my family. It bypasses some but landed in me. But no, you can't catch it."

"How did this happen?"

He tugged me back to the bed and sat, lifting me onto his lap. His arms wrapped around me, and I wondered how long I'd be able to remember this treasured feeling. Not long enough.

"Many generations ago, before most of us remember, a scientist in my family conducted experiments. He gave himself some kind of disease in the process. Since he recovered and lived for more years, loving his mate and her bearing his young, they thought nothing of the disease. Until it hit him. He wasn't stopped until he'd murdered three others."

"I'm sorry. It sounds horrible."

"He killed his sister and mother. His mate and young barely escaped his grasp." The horror in Venge's voice shot through me, making my hands shake. "They thought it was over when he died until . . ."

"Someone else in your family did the same thing." I could see where this was going, and I could understand why he'd fear the same would happen to him.

"Every three generations, the malformation is passed down. Unless the person comes here until the end and we follow the process laid out many generations ago, this person goes on a rampage and kills. Here, at least, we can be watched. Ressard's family have been the care-takers of the castle and my family for longer than anyone remembers. Him remaining here is a sacrifice someone in each third generation makes for my family."

"Why do they do it?"

"Because one of his ancestors was in the lab with mine. His ancestor helped mine experiment with the plant."

It was almost too much to believe, but I could tell Venge was telling me the truth. Was this any better now that I knew? Not really.

"We'll look for doctors who can help you," I said, determined to find another way. There had to be one, and we'd seek it until we ended this for him and every generation to come.

"I've looked. I've sought everyone, even those who offer things no one else would consider. There is no cure, and the disease will soon claim me."

"You seem fine. How do you know you have this genetic malformation?"

As the sun slipped down, hiding beneath the horizon, he held out his arm.

It had turned into stone.

I gulped, wishing I could pretend this wasn't happening.

He held me, kissed me. If there was time, I'd beg him to love me again. I could understand this, but I'd never accept it. There was no accepting his looming death.

"I have to leave soon," he finally said. "I'm sorry."

I climbed off his lap and tugged my dress over my

head with haste. "I have something you need to see. Will you wait here?" It was just a hunch on my part, but . . .

He nodded.

Opening the door, I paused and turned. "What's a true mate?"

He tugged his shirt apart, revealing the symbol I'd seen before. "This, the korier symbol. It appeared when I met you, showing me you are my mate. If we were *true* mates, you would have the same symbol as well."

I didn't have anything like that.

He must've seen me gulp. "True mates are rare. So few, no one remembers when the last true mating took place. A male is often gifted with the symbol but rarely their true mate."

True mate was mentioned in Tellesandrus's journal. I couldn't remember the exact specifics, but I suspected it might come into play with Venge. Maybe this clue could save him—save us.

"Wait. I'll be right back." I raced from his room to mine, dragging the journal out from beneath the mattress.

When I nearly tripped over the vine rope that I'd made in the meadow, I paused. Unsure why, I grabbed it and brought it with me.

But when I returned to Venge's room, he was gone. Some subtle sound drew me to a window facing the back lawn.

Venge and Ressard crossed the back lawn, heading for the woods. Before he followed Ressard into the forest,

Venge turned, looking up. Stark pain and acceptance crossed his face.

Through my tear-filled eyes, I watched as he lifted his hand. I pressed my palm against the glass as if in this final way and time, we could touch.

"I love you," he mouthed, and I felt his heady emotions sink into my bones.

"It's not enough," I said as he turned and entered the woods. There would never be enough for us unless we were together forever.

I grabbed the book and rushed from the room.

31
VENGE

Before I left her, I'd strode back and forth in front of the bank of windows, waiting with hope for Jenny to return. She'd said she had something to show me. While I didn't know what it was, if she felt it was important, it would be.

"You must leave."

I turned to find Ressard standing behind me, having entered through the rooms beyond mine.

"I have time," I said, struggling not to give into desperation.

I also struggled not to give into the gargoyle lurking within me. I sensed that part of me waiting to seize my mind and body, to take over completely.

Then there would be nothing left of Venge.

Each night, I fought the change, permitting my body to harden to flexible stone, the horns to jut from my forehead, my claws to elongate, and the wings to sprout from my back.

Each night, I allowed this to happen while holding onto my mind. That was mine, and I wouldn't let go.

But each night, it got harder to hold on. My ancestors must've gone through the same struggle. Over the last few nights, I'd lost myself before morning. Only dawn brought me back. Soon, the morning light wouldn't make a difference.

Everyone had succumbed, proving I would as well.

I wouldn't go down without a battle. Remaining here meant I could be with Jenny. Giving in meant I'd lose her.

"I am waiting here for her," I said. "She has something to show me."

He pointed to my arm that remained completely stone. "It is too late. The sun has not yet set, and you are already losing control." He swallowed and despair filled his eyes. "If I could stop this, friend, I would do so. You know this."

I braced his shoulders. "I understand." From the time I was born, and he was chosen to be here with me through my final days, I knew this moment would come. Fighting it would not keep it from happening.

"If you remain here, waiting for her, can you hold on?"

He meant, could I keep from fully changing and murdering her? I thought long and hard about this, not liking that I wasn't completely certain I could keep the gargoyle from shoving me aside.

"I want to see her one last time," I said hoarsely.

"Can you hold on?" he repeated, his face stoic. He

would not make this decision for me; I must do so myself.

Did I dare risk this?

Before my eyes, my left arm turned to stone. Always, I'd released it, essentially giving my body over to the gargoyle while holding onto my mind. The beast had never taken control on its own.

"It is different now, is it not?" Ressard said. "I am sorry. I hoped you would go into remission, that this could be held off indefinitely. I see how much you love her and how she loves you."

She did. I could *feel* it in my soul. We were mates; nothing could come between this.

Except the gargoyle waiting to claim me.

Would I be able to hold onto my mind this time?

My eyes burned with tears. I wanted more with her, but it wasn't to be.

My heart shattered.

When it was over, would I still remember her? I hoped so. I wanted to take her with me wherever I journeyed once I'd passed.

I gave him a curt nod, unable to speak, and waved to the door he'd entered through.

We'd take the back stairs, locking them behind us.

Azareela met us in the last room, tears trailing down her face. She rushed to me and gave me a hug, holding me like she'd done when I was small, and my mother rejected me.

"Son." In every way that counted, she was my true mother. "I am terribly sorry." She leaned back in my embrace. "I would take your place for you if I could. You have your life left to live, a life with your Jenny."

"It is not to be," I said dully. Pain kept crashing through me, within my heart and inside my limbs. I fought to keep the gargoyle from solidifying. I didn't dare give my body over to its command until I was chained and couldn't hurt my friends.

"We must go," Ressard said with deep sympathy.

"Where will you take him?" Azareela gulped out before holding up her palm. "No. It is cowardly of me, but I do not want to know." She turned to Ressard. "Be swift yet gentle."

He tapped his forehead. "I can do no less for a friend."

I hated that we three were bound together in this. I would die; there was no avoiding that, but my friends would have to live on, remembering their role in this.

It wasn't fair, but there was no way of avoiding it. My fate had been set many generations ago when my ancestor took a horrifying chance.

All of us paid the price for his foolhardy actions.

Azareela hugged me one last time before stepping back. She watched as we left the last room and entered the stairwell at the end of the hall.

A click resounded, showing she'd locked the door behind us.

I heard her sobs and pictured her stepping inside a room and collapsing, remaining there until it was finally over.

We left the castle and hurried across the back lawn as

the sun slipped lower. By then, one of my legs had succumbed, changing like my arms.

Before we entered a little-used path in the woods, I glanced back.

Jenny stood at my bedroom window.

32
JENNY

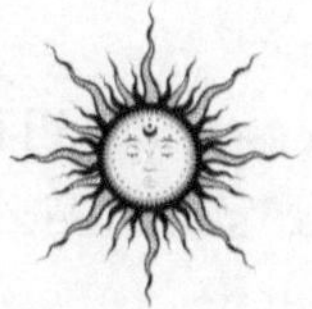

Outside Venge's room, I paused on the smooth carpet. I shouldn't take the front stairs, not when the back would bring me to the lowest level.

My heart aflame, I rushed to the other end of the hall. The door was locked.

I pivoted and raced down the hall but stopped when Azareela entered the hall from one of the rooms ahead.

"Please go to your room," she said in a jerky voice. Like me, tears covered her face. We both mourned Venge, but unlike her, I wasn't going to give up. I wouldn't allow it to end like this. There had to be a way to stop it from happening.

"I'm going to him," I said, my chin lifting.

"You cannot. You must allow this to finish."

"I'm not allowing Venge to die." I lifted my chin. "He told me everything."

She sighed. "He should have kept it secret. But if you

know the truth, then you know he must die. The beast is poised to take over. We will humanely end this for him."

"Murder him you mean."

She sniffed. "You think I do not love him as much as you? I raised that youngling as my own. I sacrificed everything to be his mother. I came here to help give him the best for his final days."

"Yet you'll allow Ressard to kill him."

"There is no choice," she shouted. "Do you not see?"

"There's always a choice."

I ran into his room and slammed the door, then locked it to keep her from entering.

What could I do?

The book lay on the bed where I'd left it. While I was desperate to find a way out of the castle to follow, I needed to read those last few lines. There was a clue there I hadn't seen the first time, and I would find it.

It would make a difference for us, I knew it.

I scrambled through the pages, quickly finding the last with writing.

I will hide this book, hoping . . . find it. There is hope. Only with her in my life can I . . . it.

Trust in your true mate. It is the cure. You . . . need . . . die.

"Trust in your true mate," I whispered, staring forward. "The true mate, also known as the korier symbol is the cure." And the last must be . . . "You do not need to die."

I read it a couple more times until I was sure I'd memorized it.

Azareela rattled the knob. "Let me in. We can mourn together."

I thought she had the codes to all the doors, but maybe not this one. Since other doors led to this room, I didn't trust her not to find another way to get to me. She'd hold me back when I needed to fly—figuratively.

One question remained. How was I getting out of here without her coming after me?

I ran to the window on the far left of the wall and, squeezing my eyes shut, begged whatever fate existed to help me open it.

It lifted easily.

"Yes," I breathed.

A glance outside showed I was very close to one of the towers only a floor below. I grabbed my vine rope and created a loop that would hold even if I put my full weight on it.

Fortunately, the tower roofs each had three small spikes. Would they support me? Only one way to find out.

Leaning out the window, I swung the rope toward the tower, but I missed a spike.

"Let me in," Azareela cried. "Please."

I tried to hook one of the spikes again. Over and over until frustration and dismay boiled inside me.

I was about to give up and find another way out when I snagged the loop on a spike. A tug showed it was solid, and I scrambled out the window. Using the rope to help maintain my balance, I inched along the narrow ledge jutting out of the wall at this floor's level.

When I was beneath the tower, I gulped and began to climb, using the rope to pull myself up onto the sloped tile surface.

Once there, I caught my breath and did not look down. I'd done this a few times to escape from my father's house when I was younger, but I'd never enjoyed heights. Looking down from twelve floors would do me in.

With my coiled rope in hand, I eased around the tower and moved as fast as I dared to the other side of the building. I hooked the rope around another spike, this one not on a tower but from the main roof itself, then used it to climb down beyond the floor where Azareela waited.

I lifted a window and climbed inside, hurrying across a dusty bedroom to the door. Cracking the door, I peeked out, finding the hall empty.

I hurried to the end and tested the door to the back stairwell.

Unlocked. Yay.

It didn't take long to reach the ground floor. I burst outside and raced across the back lawn to the woods, not stopping when I hit the narrow trail Venge and Ressard had taken. I had to trust they'd stick to it, though I'd jog slowly enough so I could look for signs they'd left the trail to strike out in another direction.

There was enough information in the lines I'd memorized, when combined with what I'd learned from Venge, to help. I knew it.

Tellesandrus hid the book, hoping the next in his

family claimed by the disease would find the journal. Why not leave it out in the open?

Maybe he worried Ressard's family wouldn't believe his words. Or maybe there was some other reason I couldn't determine. It didn't matter.

I didn't have an answer, but I'd found something that might save Venge.

I jogged for a long time, heartened to see compressions in the grass, showing someone had passed here recently.

The sun set, and it was all I could do to follow the trail.

Desperation filled me. I had information. I wasn't sure how I could use it, but I had to reach Venge before Ressard killed him. I couldn't let that happen.

My steps slowed. I wanted to run, but I had to make sure I didn't lose their trail.

The path abruptly ended at the base of an enormous cliff. I stared up, wondering where to go next.

Horror filled me. Would I stand here while Venge died?

Subtle voices reached me. No, *one* voice. Ressard.

His words were followed by a familiar bellow of pain. It had scared me the first time I heard it.

Now it sunk into me like a knife, severing something vital inside me. It was Venge. It had always been him. He was the beast I'd seen in the dungeon.

I hurried toward Ressard's voice. I wasn't too late, not as long as Venge lived.

A dark cave opening in the cliff loomed ahead. I

slowed, keeping my steps light, and paused near the opening.

"I'm sorry, friend," Ressard said. "It is time."

It wasn't time. It would never be the time for Venge to die.

I found a rock on the floor and lifted it. Then I rushed into the cave, running toward lights I spied ahead. I arrived at a barred room. Venge—now in the beastly, gargoyle-like form—was chained by his arms and legs to the back wall.

Ressard advance toward Venge, a long blade in his hand.

He lifted it as I rushed toward them.

33

VENGE

I hung onto my mind by a thread.

I was only vaguely aware of someone else entering the cell located in the back of the cave. From the old dried blood I'd seen on the floor, I wasn't the first—nor would I be the last—to die here.

I no longer lamented that this wasn't fair, that I needed more time.

All I could focus on was clinging to the scrap of what made me Venge. I couldn't let the gargoyle take over completely.

"Stop," someone cried out. "You don't need to do this."

"You must leave," another person said. "Please. You do not want to see this."

I dangled from the chains, repeating the same words over and over. *Hold on. Hold on. Hold on.* I could do it and tomorrow, I'd get to see Jenny again. Anything was worth one moment holding her in my arms.

"You're not going to hurt him," the person said.

I opened blurry eyes and watched, stunned, as Jenny grappled with Ressard, struggling to gain control of the knife.

"I can help him," she cried, giving up and backing away from Ressard.

She scooted around him and approached me.

"Go," I struggled to bite out. My entire body had been consumed by the gargoyle, and it was all I could do to keep a grip on the tiny bit of me left.

"I found a journal," she yelled. "It was Tellesandrus's."

"What?" Ressard asked, lowering the blade to his side.

"There's a way to cure Venge," she said.

I shook my head, my horns banging on the stone wall. "It's not possible," I said thickly. My tongue didn't want to work. Nothing would work.

"It has to be," she said, her desperate gaze meeting mine. "Let me tell you."

That's when I felt the gargoyle wrench my mind away from me.

That's when I knew I couldn't stop this any longer.

34
JENNY

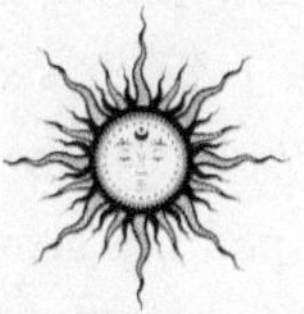

"I do not understand," Ressard said.

Venge growled and thrashed, trying to break free from the wall. His bellows of pain echoed around us, making it hard to think. But I had to get through to Ressard.

I had an idea.

"Unchain him," I yelled.

"No. He will kill you."

"He won't. He loves me. I love him. I know he won't hurt me."

I backed toward Venge, who stopped struggling and sniffed as if scenting me.

With a groan, he growled and strained, trying to break free. His wings smacked against the wall, and his horns slashed through the air. His claws were twice their original length.

"He has been consumed," Ressard said, his body slumping. "He is gone."

"He isn't." I knew Venge was still with me.

I could *feel* him. His love encircled me like his warm arms. I just needed to show Ressard.

Ressard's hand snapped out, but I backed away, right up against Venge.

My back hit his chest, and he stilled, staring down at me with glowing eyes. I didn't see my love there, but I knew in my heart—my soul—he was still with me.

I turned and wrapped my arms around him. "I love you, Venge. Come back to me. Please."

The beast stilled and dropped his big stone head to sniff my hair.

His growl turned to a whine, and tears sprang to my eyes.

"I love you," I said again. "Come back to me, Venge. We have so much to live for."

The back of my right hand burned, and I tugged it out from behind him to see why.

"A korier symbol," I said with joy tainted with fear. "A korier symbol." I leaned back and looked up at Venge.

The gargoyle's gaze met mine.

I showed him my hand. "Look, Venge. We're true mates. I'm yours, and you're mine." I recited the last lines of the book, inserting words I believed had been smeared by water. "I will hide this book, hoping future generations can find it. There is hope. Only with her in my life can I survive it. Trust in your true mate. It is the cure. You do not need to die."

"I don't understand," Ressard said, frowning. "How can a true mating be a cure?"

"I have a korier symbol," I said, watching Venge. "I am your true mate."

He stared at me for a long while . . .

. . . Then he shifted back into himself.

35
VENGE

"This is not possible," Ressard said, stomping closer. "Once night falls, the beast consumes him until dawn. What has changed?"

I'd only heard the last bit of what Jenny said, enough to know she was my true mate. My korier heart. The one I would love for this lifetime and beyond.

"Release me," I groaned, my body trembling. I could feel the gargoyle inside me, but the menace I'd always sensed was gone.

"This cannot be happening," Ressard said as Jenny clung to my chest, kissing my skin. "It is not possible."

"The gargoyle is still with me, but . . ." I shook my head, not sure how to explain. Something had changed, and I sensed that part of my life was over. I would not need to die, because the beast . . . was me. And I was him. "We are one."

"You don't have to die," Jenny whispered against my skin. "You don't have to die." She backed away, placing herself between me and Ressard. "Where are Tellesan-drus and his true mate's bodies?"

"He killed her. Himself after," Ressard said with complete certainty.

"One of your ancestors saw this happen?" I asked, understanding where Jenny was taking this.

"Of course not, but everyone knows this," he said. "He killed her, and then ended his own life before my ancestor could do it for him."

"So, there were never bodies found," Jenny said with anger. "Your family made assumptions."

He shrugged. "What else was my ancestor supposed to believe? The beast had always taken control. He had killed until we ended his life. All know this. So, it has been in the past, and so it will be forever."

"He didn't kill her or himself," Jenny said with complete confidence. "His true mate cured him, just as me being Venge's true mate has brought about a chemical reaction inside him that has allowed him to control the beast." She looked back at me, tears sparkling in her eyes. "That's what happened, isn't it? You can feel the gargoyle, but it's no longer struggling for control."

"You are correct." I was humbled by her words, her love, and grateful I'd found her. She'd not only saved my life, but she'd also saved us.

"A true mate's love is the cure for the disease," I said. "Jenny is my true mate." I rattled the chains. "Release me."

"I cannot," Ressard said sadly. "You will change back and kill."

"I control this," I bellowed.

While Ressard stared in disbelief, I closed my eyes and willed the change. I could feel my skin hardening, turning to a flexible stone.

Ressard gasped.

Jenny tightened her arms around me and kissed my chest.

Just as quickly as I'd turned into the gargoyle, I changed back to myself.

"Do you need another demonstration?" I growled.

"No," Ressard said weakly. "You . . . it cannot be possible, but it is." His gaze took in Jenny. "I thank you. You have saved him. I did not wish to end my friend's life."

He rushed forward and released me from the wall.

"Your poor wrists and ankles," Jenny cooed, carefully stroking a finger along the abrasion on my right wrist. "We need some medicine to heal them."

"I must tell Azareela this wonderful news," Ressard said, bowing before scurrying from the cave.

"It's over," Jenny said, grinning up at me with tears streaming down her face. "It's over."

I wrapped my arms around her. With weak legs, I lowered us to the floor, taking her into my lap where I could hold her. "Not completely over. The gargoyle is now a part of me."

"You are the gargoyle but you're both my Venge." She rose onto her knees and tugged my face down for a long kiss. "You are in control, not the beast struggling to find meaning inside you."

"We have merged. We are one for always." I could tell the beast would never take over. Beast? The gargoyle didn't quite exist any longer. It lived only by my will alone. "I was severed but now I am whole. That is what it feels like, as if a part of me had been walled off and now it has combined with my soul."

"We know the cure," she said. "There will be future generations, but we will help them find their true mates. They will know from the moment they're born that they don't have to die. They will live just as you can now live."

"You saved me, mate." I lifted her hand and kissed her korier symbol. "You and your love."

36

EPILOGUE: JENNY

ix Weeks Later

S We left the planet and the castle, unsure if us or any of Venge's future generations would ever return. The ship took us to Venge's home planet, where his family greeted him at first with reservation, but then with love. I was met with skepticism that soon turned to happiness. Saving his life with my obvious love for him helped win friends.

Azareela journeyed with us, as did the culairs. Ressard chose to remain at the castle, feeling he had a duty to maintain and keep it ready for anyone who chose to visit.

We spent a few days at each estate Venge owned until picking a favorite to move into. He'd inherited the wealth collected by the other gargoyles who'd come before him. When he was born, it was placed in an account in his name to be used to work on the castle or live on until the beast started to take over. The intent was to hold the wealth for the next person.

We'd set up a trust for anyone who might be taken by the disease, though now that we knew the cure, we were confident no one else would be killed. We'd make sure they found their true mates and that they knew what needed to be done to live.

One afternoon, we decided to take a picnic lunch to an isolated location behind one of Venge's estates. I had a surprise for him, and he said he wanted to experiment with his gargoyle form.

My skin tingled at the thought of what he'd come up with. He could seamlessly shift, and since he was still the guy I loved inside whatever "suit" he chose to wear, we played around with him in both. I had two lovers wrapped up in one male.

Fleese and Gular danced along with us. They'd grown, the tops of their backs coming to my waist. I'd read they'd be taller than Venge when they were fully mature.

The sun shone down, and Venge's hand was warm around mine.

I smiled up at him. "Love you."

"Mate." He stopped and lowered the picnic basket to the ground. While the culairs chased this planet's version of butterflies across the field, Venge tugged me close. He lifted me so our mouths could meet.

As always, heat burst inside me. I wanted him all the time, and he felt the same, to the dismay of his family who'd come to visit. We kept skipping out on them to be alone.

The symbol on my hand blazed like inner sparks flitted around the outside of the circle. I still marveled that it had appeared on my skin, but I was eternally grateful it had. Without it, I wasn't sure I could've saved Venge. Although, love was a powerful thing, I believed I could've broken through his beast side to find the guy I loved no matter what.

He lowered me to my feet, and we continued walking.

However, we stopped when we spied a small space-ship sitting on the ground ahead.

"Wait here," Venge said with a frown, handing me the picnic basket. He strode closer to the ship as the hatch opened.

The culairs tiptoed behind him like guard dogs, their spiked tails jutting into the air. I wouldn't put it past them to attack if they felt as though Venge or I were being threatened.

Even Fleese would jump to Venge's defense. When we returned from the cave, Fleese raced right up to Venge and whimpered for pats. We suspected the conflict churning within Venge spooked him and that held him back. Seeing Venge as one person now no longer fright-ened Fleese.

I couldn't be happier about it. We weren't sure what we would've done if Fleese hadn't warmed up, though I'd still had a few pet whisperer tricks up my sleeve.

Venge spoke with the male who stepped out of the ship, then waved for me to come closer.

"I am Thrombuka," the alien male said. "Throm to my friends, please." He bowed while I checked him out in a mostly clinical way. His golden skin peeking from his rolled-up shirt sleeves, his face gleaming in the sunshine like he was a god molded out of gold and plunked down in our back field. Pale lavender highlights wove through his almost white hair he wore tied at the back of his neck. A few strands lifted in the breeze, showing me when he released it, it would hang halfway down his back.

He was the same height as Venge, though he had a slightly more muscular build. Thick brown horns coiled up across his head, curling down beside his ears.

I held out my hand. "I'm Jenny."

His pale blue eyes caught mine, and I dragged them away, my skin tingling. He was hot, but he could never compete with Venge. Still, I couldn't hold back my grin. If he wasn't with anyone already, someone was going to soon snatch him up. Hot guys like him didn't remain single for long.

Venge smiled and winked at me, teasing me about being disconcerted about another male. This was one more thing I loved about my mate; he was never jealous. I was his and he was mine, and if death and a raging gargoyle couldn't break us up, there was no one in the universe who could come between us.

"I was lost and stopped to see if someone could give me guidance," Throm said. "I will soon compete in a competition that will decide who will cater Crown Prince

Lordenfeer's glorious wedding, when he will formally matebond with an Earthling. Royalty from numerous planets will be in attendance. I hope I shall win, as the competition will decide who will cater the feast to celebrate their mating."

"It sounds like a wonderful contest," I said. From what I'd heard, Interstellar Chef was not only entertaining but deadly for the contestants. The prize might be amazing, but Throm was brave to risk losing his life in a cooking competition.

Throm dipped his head. "It would be the crowning achievement of my career as a chef. I will do almost anything to ensure I am the victor."

"Venge and I are planning our wedding, too, though it won't be anything as fancy as the prince's, just a simple service with friends and family." A few of my friends would travel from Earth to attend. My father and Thurston were not invited, though my mom said she was determined to come. I couldn't wait to see her. I planned to talk her into remaining here and never going back to Earth.

Throm's gaze traveled between me and Venge and settled on the korier symbol shimmering on the back of my hand. "I wish you the best with your wedding and your life together. I . . ." He shook his head and tightened his spine. "I met my fated mate in the past but I lost her."

My eyes widened. "Lost?" How was that possible?

"I was with her but called away. After that, I couldn't find her."

The sorrow on his face made an ache bloom in my chest. "I hope you find her again."

"As do I. Males of my species rarely find true love."

I leaned into Venge's side. "Being with your true love is the most wonderful thing in the world."

Throm nodded, envy alight in his face.

"You were looking for directions?" I asked, not wanting to make him feel worse. But he had to leave, and I was eager to get on with the day I'd planned with Venge.

The culairs hung back, sniffing the air, and Throm kept shooting them frowns, though he didn't appear frightened by the beasts.

"Yes," he said. "The first event takes place soon, though I'm expected to make an appearance at the arena for introductions. Each event will be held in a different location to feature that culture's cuisine. The first competition will take place in the jungle of Trillaphon."

I couldn't imagine cooking in a jungle, but I'd be happy to watch. Maybe we'd be able to pick up the streamed vid here.

"Trillaphon can be found in the Wondron Sector," Venge said. "But you need to go to the arena first. I know of it and can show you on your com, if you'd like." He pointed to the device strapped to Throm's right wrist.

Throm held the com up. "Thank you."

It didn't take Venge long to lock the location for Throm. He returned to his ship with a wave and a flash of his tusks, and the ship took off, soaring toward the sky.

"Poor guy," I said. "I hope he finds his mate again."

Venge stroked my hair off my face. "I would be lost without you, mate. I cannot imagine the pain he must feel."

We kissed, our breathing getting heavy and our hearts racing.

With shared, heady smiles, we grabbed the basket, hugged the culairs to reassure them, and continued toward the hill where we'd hold our picnic.

Once we arrived, we sat on the blanket I'd spread out and ate a variety of yummy things grown on Venge's estate. After, we laid back and watched the clouds drift by overhead.

"You had something to tell me?" Venge said, turning to face me. He propped his head on his palm, his elbow compressing the grass.

When I found out, it was all I could do to keep the news secret. I wanted to share it when we were alone, which wasn't as often as I'd like.

"I'm—"

Fleese galloped over with Gular on his tail and nudged Venge's hip. It might be a love nudge, but it shifted Venge forward. He laughed and rolled onto his back. Fleese started nuzzling Venge's neck, whining and fussing while giving culair kisses.

Gular grunted and trotted around us to find my neck, determined to take part in the lovefest.

The tickle of his snout made me giggle, and I was soon rolling around with the beast, giving him lots of pats and hugs.

The culairs were distracted by a bird landing on the

other side of the small field and raced toward it. The bird took flight, and the culairs stared up at it, whining for it to come back. They only wanted to play.

"You were saying?" Venge said, grinning my way.

I loved seeing him so carefree, as if the weight of the world no longer held him down. He'd relaxed since we left the castle, and I couldn't love him more.

"I better spit it out before Fleese and Gular interrupt again."

He nodded, his gaze gliding along my frame with appreciation.

"We're going to have a youngling," I said, my smile widening. "I'm pregnant."

"Mate," he breathed. He cupped my face and kissed me with so much tenderness, it made tears spring up in my eyes. "You make me complete."

"Keep that in mind when our youngling is screaming in the middle of the night and needs a diaper change," I said with a laugh.

"I will change all the deepers."

"I'm holding you to that as a promise."

He stood. "You can rely on me."

I joined him, hugging him. "There's no one else I could trust more."

He grumbled and huffed, but I could tell by his smile that my words pleased him. He'd worried for a time that he'd be unable to control his shift to the gargoyle and that the horrifying process would start again, but he'd remained in control. He could change at will, though he didn't take on the gargoyle form very often. Over time, I believed he'd become more comfortable with that side of himself.

And I secretly wondered what it would be like to have sex with him in that form, though I hadn't told him. Not until he fully embraced everything he was inside.

"I have noticed you staring with lust at me when I am in my gargoyle form," he said, surprising me with his insight.

I squeaked. "You have?" I thought I'd kept it hidden.

"And that is my surprise."

"Oh," I said coyly, teasing a finger down his arm. "Would you care to share more?"

He backed up and stripped off his clothing. We were completely alone here; he'd determined that when we arrived.

"You next," he said in a husky voice.

Oh, my.

It didn't take me long to tug off my dress and toss it aside.

With his cock a stiff rod already, he changed into his gargoyle form. His glowing eyes met mine, his over-flowing with love.

His wings spread wide as if he tested them, and when he held out his arms, I ran to him, jumping and wrapping my legs around him. I loved how firm yet supple his body was in this form. I'd secretly ached to feel him licking me while I held onto his horns.

And his wings . . .

"Can you fly?" I asked.

"We're about to find out," he growled with a heady smile. Even his voice was different in this form.

He soared up into the sky, jerky at first. He confessed he'd snuck out many times at night to learn how to control himself in flight. I loved that he'd embraced this part of himself.

"This is amazing," I cried as we flew over a vast forest.

"There's something else amazing I'd like to try." He stared down at me with pure lust in his eyes. "What do you think of mid-flight sex?"

"Venge," I said with a grin. "I thought you'd never ask."

Do you miss Venge & Jenny already?
You can catch up with them one last time
in a bonus epilogue – It's time for their wedding!
Just sign up for my newsletter
& I'll send you a copy.
SIGN ME UP!

If you enjoyed Venge & Jenny's story,
could you leave a review?
I'd love to hear your thoughts.

Join Throm & Wren as they compete

in the bakeoff of the century

in Catering to the Alien.

It's the *Hunger Games* meets *Chopped*.

You can read the first chapter here.

Just turn the page . . .

SERIES BY AVA

Mail-Order Brides of Crakair

Brides of Driegon

Fated Mates of the Ferlaern Warriors

Fated Mates of the Xilan Warriors

Holiday with a Cu'zod Warrior

Galaxy Games

Alien Warrior Abandoned/
Shattered Galaxies

Beastly Alien Boss

You can find my books on Amazon.

ABOUT THE AUTHOR

Ava Ross is a *USA Today* Bestselling author of numerous titles. She fell for men with unusual features when she first watched Star Wars, where alien creatures have gone mainstream. She lives in New England with her husband (who is sadly not an alien, though he is still cute in his own way), her kids, and a few assorted pets.

CATERING TO THE ALIEN

**It's the cooking contest of a lifetime.
I just need to avoid falling for a hot alien chef.**

To raise credits for the local creature shelter, I enter Interstellar Chef. If I win? I'm awarded the catering job of a lifetime and prize money I can donate to the shelter. It won't be easy—contestants must prepare exquisite meals in dangerous alien locations and fellow chefs have been known to attack the others. Some competitors don't make it home alive.

All I have to do is avoid my stiffest competition, Thrombuka Nargoth, the brutishly handsome, golden-skinned alien who once left me stranded without my undies in a secluded hallway of a dive bar on Quazar 3.

Fraternization among the competitors is strictly forbidden, but the more I try to avoid Throm, the more I can't resist him. Soon we're stealing kisses away from the prying eyes of the camera bots. If we're caught, we'll get thrown off the show.

Fate has other plans, however, and soon I don't know what I'm fighting for most—the prize money for the shelter or a future with Throm.

Catering to the Alien is Book 3 in the Beastly Alien Boss Series. Each features an Earth woman hired for an off-world job who meets a gruff alien who can't resist falling for his fated mate.

CHAPTER 1
WREN

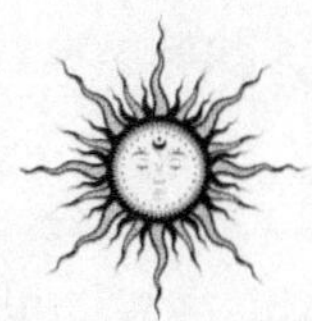

"Someone's staring at you," one of my friends said, nudging her head toward a corner of the dive bar in Viskius, the biggest city on Quazar 3.

We sat at a high-top table, nursing the drinks we'd ordered when we arrived.

As one of the chefs on an interstellar cruise, I didn't often take advantage of the chance to visit one of the ports the ship docked into throughout the galaxy, but a few of my fellow staff members invited me to go with them to Quazar 3 on our night off.

I'd shrugged and hopped into the transport shuttle with them, planning to have a couple of drinks, then return to the ship. I was scheduled for breakfast duty, which meant I needed to hop out of bed at four o'clock sharp.

I started to turn to see *who* was looking, but Faliera hissed, her forked tongue flicking out. She laid one of her four hands on my arm. "Play hard to get. Play hard to get!"

"I *am* hard to get." Spontaneity was not my middle name. I dated, but only after checking out a guy's resume. Well, not exactly. But I had been known to ask his friends about him before accepting a guy's invitation.

"If you look, you signal you're interested," Faliera said.

"Maybe I am?"

"He's still looking this way," Juliest said, followed by a high-pitched gurgling giggle. This ruffled the flaps on her neck gills and made her face turn scarlet.

"Oh, my," gasped Faliera. Her tail shot up toward her back, nearly hitting an alien walking past our table. "Don't look!"

I nudged aside the hovering drink menu that kept zooming in close to my face, suggesting I order another. "But you just said—"

"Shh." Her lavender eyes widened, and her voice dropped off to almost nothing. "He's coming this way."

Trying not to be obvious about it, I'd glanced around, spying a golden-skinned alien standing close behind me with a tusk-baring smile on his face that made my knees melt faster than biergart fat in a sizzling hot frying pan.

My gaze locked with his, and while I fumbled to find something witty to say, he extended his hand my way.

"Allow me to introduce myself," he said with a dip of his head. He wore his nearly white hair with pale lavender streaks secured at the nape of his neck. The thick strands dangled halfway down his back. His bronze horns coiled across the top of his head, the blunted tips nearly touching his shoulders. "I'm Thrombuka Durvanak Nargoth. Throm for short."

Who introduces themselves by using their complete name anymore? Still, he sounded sincere. And I was a sucker for guys with pale blue eyes and taller-than-my-five-ten muscular frames, let alone tusks and horns.

"Can I buy you another drink?" he asked, nudging his chin to my nearly empty glass.

"Sure." I practically breathed the word. I could barely think with his skin touching mine.

One of the other women tittered.

I swallowed and tried to come up with something intelligent to say. Now would not be a good time to ask him for references.

He hailed the hover-menu and put in our order. "While we wait, would you like to dance?"

Dance? "Oh, um, yeah." I stood, and he kept hold of my hand, leading me out onto the dancefloor, a scrap of pleenar wood with barely enough room to sway around on.

Since he was at least a head-and-a-half taller than me, he lifted me up to bring me to eye level. My feet dangled. The only way to make this work was to wrap my legs around his waist and grab onto his shoulders. This should've put me well above anything hard down south unless the guy was big and long.

My eyes popped when I felt something shifting against my groin.

He shot me a grin, but when I spied a touch of

shyness on his face, I relaxed. So he had a stiffy. That was a good sign, right?

We swayed around until the dance came to an end.

"Thanks," I said.

"Thank you." He grinned, and damn, tusks. I'd always wondered what it would feel like to kiss a guy with tusks.

With the light buzz from my first drink loosening my inhibitions, I decided to find out. I leaned forward and planted my lips on his. His tusks didn't hurt. In fact, they felt sensual rubbing against my upper lip

I'd read about heat searing through a woman's veins, of being suddenly desperate to be with someone from one touch alone, and of aching to rip off clothing to feel skin on skin.

No one had brought this out of me until I kissed Throm.

I had a feeling I'd been missing out on all the fun stuff.

In seconds, we'd left the dance floor. He carried me down the hall, his lips still locked on mine.

I groaned and rubbed against him, not caring if my coworkers saw me. Not caring that I barely knew this brutish alien. I hadn't even quizzed one of his friends.

The back of the hall curved to the right, then dead-ended at a closet. With one big, clawed hand gripping my ass, he yanked the door open with the other and hauled out a lonely broom and mop resting against the back wall, tossing them onto the floor of the hallway.

We tumbled inside. The door banged shut as he

pressed me against the wall, lifting me and grinding himself against me.

A fever charged through my cells, linking them together. Nothing would satisfy me other than feeling his long, thick, glorious cock buried deep within me. Whimpering, I tore at his clothing while he yanked down my pants.

"Bend forward, luscious," Throm growled, pivoting me around. "Your lips are sweeter than hoolig, and I need a taste of everything else you have to offer."

"Someone might see," I said, heat climbing into my cheeks. Truly, though, did it matter? He'd kissed me out of my inhibitions, my undies, and my willpower. There was nothing stopping him from claiming me other than his dark leather pants.

He leaned me forward and stooped down between my legs, parting my thighs. I was dripping already.

Someone knocked on the door, the sound barely breaking through my overwhelming lust.

"Ignore it," I cried, shimmying closer to his face. I'd sacrifice anything to feel his tongue gliding inside me.

He stood and cracked the door, shielding me from view with his body, and spoke to whoever stood on the other side in a tone too low for me to hear what they said.

Throm shut the door. Frustration gleamed in his eyes, and his hard cock kicked against the front of his pants. "I'll be right back."

"What?" I asked.

"Hold that pose," he said with a low, husky chuckle,

stroking my bare ass with a claw. "I promise. I won't be long."

He slipped out of the closet.

And that was the last time I saw Thrombuka Durvanak Nargoth.

One Interstellar Year Later

"You're fired," my boss snarled, her four suction cup-covered limbs flailing in the air. One smacked on the grill and sizzled, but she was so angry, she didn't appear to notice. "If you will not work all night, you will leave the premises immediately."

I ducked to keep from being hit by one of her longer upper limbs. She wasn't vicious—not usually—but when she was pissed off, she could be unpredictable. There was no need for me to see stars after a blow to the head. Been there, done that once already. It sucked working with a blinding headache.

My boss was in an uproar because I'd refused to work when my shift was finished. I'd been here twelve hours already. Exhausted after working in the kitchen alone all day, my eyes stung, and my arms had turned into lead poles dangling at my sides.

"Please don't fire me," I said, struggling to sound reasonable. "Think of the creatures."

This was actually my second job. The first paid for my tiny room here on the space station and food/essentials. This part-time job generated a small check I donated each lunar cycle to the local creature shelter.

It was too common for ships to dock at the space station and dump the pet they'd brought with them. Like they thought someone would scoop the poor creature up and adopt them. Nope. I found many wandering the bowels of the station with hunger and desolation in their eyes. The shelter found them loving forever homes.

However, it wasn't easy to find decent chefs on a space station. My boss needed me more than I needed her.

She pressed her flat, gray face close to mine. "If you do not—"

My com chimed, and with relief flooding me, I held up my arm to show her I had a call.

She snarled and snapped but backed away.

I ducked into the hallway outside the kitchen and leaned against the wall, blowing stray strands of hair off my face.

When my com chimed again, I clicked into the message.

You, Wren Phillips, have been chosen to compete in the next round of Interstellar Chef!

Wait, what?

My eyes widened as I verified what I'd heard with the text. This must be a mistake. Sure, I'd applied for the position at the Interstellar Employment Agency on a whim a lunar cycle ago, but I never dreamed I'd be selected.

You will compete with four other contestants, the shrill, accented, alien voice said through my com. *The person with the lowest score each day will be eliminated from the show, and whoever wins the final round will cater the reception for the upcoming wedding of Crown Prince Lordenfeer and his illustrious Earthling bride.*

Everyone had heard about the prince and the Earth woman he'd met at the palace. Their wedding would take place in one lunar cycle. Whoever scored the catering job would be inundated with job offers from restaurants. But with the prize credits, the winner could open their own business.

This couldn't be happening. It was the chance of a lifetime. There wasn't a chef in the galaxy who wouldn't leap at the opportunity to compete on Interstellar Chef. The show was recorded and streamed throughout the multi-universe. Even the losers often received offers of employment.

Yeah, the show was purported to be dangerous, but surely everyone made it home alive. The "deaths" were staged. Right?

With the prize, I could finally leave the space station and start over in a place where my mother's shadow didn't hang over me. Just as exciting, I could donate to the creature shelter, and they'd be financially set for years.

Please confirm your receipt of this offer and interest in participating in the show, the alien voice said through my com. *And then prepare yourself to be transported to the Bres-sarian Arena for the opening event tomorrow. Since space is tight on the shuttle, you may only bring one bag. Outfits emblazoned with the show's logo will be provided for each of the events. Pack light! Pack well. And get ready for the cooking contest of a lifetime!*

Receipt confirmed, I'm in. I typed with shaky fingers. *I want to participate,* I added in case "I'm in" wasn't clear.

My heart zinged around, smacking against my ribcage. I couldn't believe it. It was all I could do not to cry.

Hey, it was time to start packing.

Well, I'd pack as soon as I finished up here.

Your transport will arrive at the space station's dock X37 to collect you promptly at 08:00 tomorrow morning. We wish you all the best in the competition.

My com bleeped as the transmittal cut out.

I danced around the hall, giggling madly.

"I'm going to win this," I kept singing.

"There you are," my boss bellowed, snaking her limbs through the kitchen doorway. Two latched onto me, and I was lifted off the tile floor and hauled into the sweltering, grease-scented room. "Get to work or you're fired." She smacked me down in front of the grill hard enough my teeth jarred together.

"You can't fire me," I said with quiet dignity. "Because I quit." I wrenched off the stained apron I'd worn since that morning while preparing delicate cuisine and tossed it at my boss. "Send my final check to the creature shelter."

She deflected the apron with a snap of a limb and stomped toward me on her four hooves. "Get out of my kitchen," she snarled.

"Alrighty, then." I lifted my chin and resisted taunting her with how she'd never find another chef who could match my delicate sauces, how she didn't know the secret ingredient I included in my fry batter, and how she had no clue how to prepare a tuskareen roast so that the meat melted off the bone.

With a big grin, I stomped from her kitchen.

Three days later, I stood in a small room at the top of the floating Bressarian Arena, fidgeting while I waited for my name to be announced for the upcoming season of Interstellar Chef.

Sweat trickled down my spine, and I wiggled in the stupid, form-fitting sparkly silver gown they'd asked me to wear for my introduction.

The arena orbited one of the small moons of Quazar 3. I hadn't returned there since the cruise, and I cringed at the idea of walking through the streets of Viskius City again.

After Throm had bailed on me, I'd pawed around inside the broom closet, but my panties were nowhere to be found. Had Throm taken them with him? Jerk.

I'd hurried back to my friends; told them I had a

headache—which I totally did—and returned to the cruise ship.

I'd given my notice the second the ship put into the space station.

At least I didn't have to go anywhere near the bar. I'd leave the arena for the first event that would take place on Trillaphon in the Wondron Sector, along with the other four competitors.

A tall, blue-skinned female who'd earlier introduced herself as Trixaine opened the door and poked one of her two small heads inside the opening. A grin split her face, stretching from one cheekbone to the other. "Are you ready, honey?" She curled one of her three fingers my way. "It's time."

I followed her from the room, my impossibly high heels clicking on the floor and the hem of my gown swishing across my ankles. I wouldn't compete in this outfit, thank the stars. Matching tunics and pants with the show's logo emblazoned across the front would be waiting in my shuttle cabin.

I felt like a thick knife. Or a silver torch. Watchers were going to be blinded by my stunning appearance —literally.

"So, honey," Trixaine said, her two heads undulating, softly bumping against each other. Her snake-like hair had been coiled up on the top of each of her heads with a gold chain linking the braids in the back. Her thick, scaled tail swayed back and forth, bumping into the walls of the narrow hallway. "When you get out there, they'll ask you some basic questions." She flashed her fangs. "Nothing too personal. This will give you a chance to show the multi-universes who you are. It's your time to shine."

As I stood beside her, cheers erupted from the arena, followed by clapping.

I sucked in a deep breath. "What should I expect out there?"

"You'll step onto an orbiting island. It will transport you up beside our very own Jell Pleecard, the Bretak nobleman who will host the season."

I'd met him this morning when he stopped by my cabin.

"He'll ask you a few very easy questions," Trixaine said. "Relax and try to sound natural when you give your answers. After that, you'll be introduced to the other competitors."

I released a heavy breath. "Good. It sounds simple."

She wrapped an arm around my shoulders and squeezed so tight I almost yelped. "Very simple. No fear. No worries. This is going to be a lot of fun."

Cooking was fun. An introduction being live streamed to trillions of aliens throughout six or eight universes?

Major cringe.

I didn't enjoy being stared at, though I supposed I'd have to get used to it since I'd be under the scrutiny of the camera bots for the next week or so, other than during my free time.

I braced myself and nodded. "I'm ready."

The door opened, and I stepped out onto the orbiting

island. I was lifted until I reached the center of the enormous arena. I'd expected stands with beings watching the opening event, but only a ton of hyper-link camera bots floated around, taking everything in from all angles.

"Welcome," Jell cried, zooming in close to me. Hover jets had fused with his lower legs, and I'd read he wore them almost all the time. "May I say, Wren, that dress looks fabulous on you. You shine!"

"Thank you," I said in the lull that followed.

Cheers erupted, making me jump, and I realized they were fake, injected into the show to make viewers believe a billion aliens were watching.

"Without further ado, let's get started, shall we?"

I pressed for a grin, but it came out weak.

"What is your favorite food?" Jell asked, nodding his head in an encouraging manner. "Just speak normally, dear. The camera bots will hear you just fine."

"My favorite food?" I said, my spine loosening. Maybe this wouldn't be too bad. The lack of audience made my spine loosen and my frayed nerves unravel. "Jujist berries."

"Ah, lovely. And spices." He wiggled the spikes on his shoulders. "Here's a tricky question. What spices would you use to enhance a limerund roast?"

My smile came easier. "Everyone knows a limerund roast is best seasoned with cardira."

"No," he gasped in mock excitement, two of his four hands cupping his bright pink cheeks. All of him was pink, actually—the parts I could see outside of his deep purple suit. "But cardira is sweet."

"Garlic and a touch of dundun cut the sweetness. It's amazing." I grinned. "You should try it sometime."

"Oh, you can be assured, I will!" His gaze moved to the closest camera bots. "Did you hear that, folks? Cardira and dundun. *Ahh.*"

A fake cheer and applause rang out while he nodded approvingly, flashing his three-inch fangs.

He asked me six more questions, each designed to make me look good. I knew this because they were all as easy as the first. I was soon relaxed and almost enjoying my introduction. I could ignore the cameras and be myself.

"Thank you," Jell finally said. "We *all* thank you! I know our viewers will have more questions, and I'll happily collect and ply them at a later date. But for now, I ask you to wait with three of your fellow chefs while I introduce the last."

My island took me over to wait with theirs.

"And the final contestant is . . ." A drumroll sounded as Jell whizzed past us on his hover jets.

A hovering island rose from below like mine had, revealing a male dressed in tight black pants and a billowy white shirt.

My breath caught.

Throm's intent gaze met mine.

Pick up your copy of
Catering to the Alien on Amazon!